Worth the Chance

A NOVEL

◆ FriesenPress

Suite 300 - 990 Fort St
Victoria, BC, Canada, V8V 3K2
www.friesenpress.com

ISBN
978-1-4602-8124-6 (Hardcover)
978-1-4602-8125-3 (Paperback)
978-1-4602-8126-0 (eBook)

1. Fiction, Christian, Romance

Distributed to the trade by The Ingram Book Company

For Ryan.

1 Corinthians 13:7

ACKNOWLEDGEMENTS

Readers! Your encouragement made this book happen. I hope you enjoy this story about a few other favourites you read about in 'Worth the Risk'.

Ryan, this would never be possible without you. Your unwavering support is a necessary ingredient to this not-so-little project, as well as my sanity. Love you.

Carly, your work is flawless, and the cover is unbelievable once again.

Alysha, I could not have chosen a more perfect cover model to be my Sophie. Thanks for playing the part!

A big thanks to my first readers of Logan and Sophie's story— your thoughts and suggestions made this story what it is.

And finally, to the Author of Life for the opportunity to tell the story You laid on my heart.

One

L OGAN Fraser smoothed his hand down the calf's back to calm her as best he could. He would be riled up too if his leg was wrapped in barbed wired, and he sat trapped, while his friends roamed the pasture. The calf jerked again, and her front legs connected with Logan's shin.

"Whoa, little one, no need to put us both on the injured list." Logan continued to stroke her back while ignoring the sharp pain traveling up his leg.

Looking again at the horizon—the direction from where his help should arrive, Logan listened for a sign that he was on the way. With cattle, it was never a one-man job. Sure enough, he heard his ranch hand's ATV in the distance. Seconds later, a silhouette popped over the hill and sped toward the fence line. It was the start of June, so there was no need for headlights after 5 o'clock in the morning. Mike slowed the vehicle and parked about a hundred feet away as not to spook the calf any more than she already was.

"Eighty-four?" Mike called while he grabbed his tools off the back of the quad.

Logan hadn't thought to check her ear tag until Mike mentioned it. When he first spotted the calf, he alerted Mike right away and began calming her down. He reached for her ear while still soothingly stroking her back.

"Good guess," he confirmed.

"Man, that's the third time. When is she going to learn that the grass isn't greener on the other side?"

Logan huffed at Mike's attempted joke. It was true though— once a runner, always a runner.

Mike dropped his tools next to the calf and kneeled down inspecting the barbed wire around her leg. The wire had cut deep enough to draw some blood, but it didn't look like it would cause any lasting damage, from what Logan had assessed earlier. She'd be an auction cow if it caused a limp later on, but with her track record for attempted escapes it wasn't looking good for her either way. Mike reached beside him for the wire cutters.

"Think she'll keep still?" he said.

The calf had relaxed considerably since Logan first found her about half an hour ago, but he didn't want to risk another kick to the shins.

"Probably not. I'll hold her, you snip."

Logan turned so his back was to the calf and leaned his body into her stomach while grabbing a hold of her front legs. She lurched and jolted, but Logan held on. He started talking to her with hopes that maybe it would take her mind off her leg and what Mike was doing.

"Hey now, Eighty-four, no reason to be scared. You'll be free in just a second. Free to run and frolic—"

"Frolic?" Mike interjected with a smirk.

Logan sent Mike a testing look, but continued, "You can find your friends and your mama. Drink as much milk and eat as much grass as you want, so you can get nice and plump before we sell you off. Isn't that right, sweetheart?"

The calf gave up a sigh and relaxed at his words.

Mike held in his laughter, but added, "If she only knew."

"Would you just get it done already?" Logan asked not wanting to risk another kick to the leg.

"Yeah, yeah. Hold your horses." Mike gently grabbed the trapped legs and held it still. He worked the wire cutters between the barbed wire and her leg slowly so not to cause further injury or agitate the cuts. With a quick snip, the wire unraveled and the calf was free.

She bolted right out from underneath Logan and took off toward the rest of the herd without a second glance at her rescuers. Logan stood and adjusted his ball cap, which had been knocked crooked from his earlier wrestling match, and watched the calf rejoin her friends.

He turned back to Mike and began repairing the fence with new barbed wire on the back of the quad. Mike strung it out between posts, and Logan tacked it on with fencing nails and a hammer. Once finished, Logan gathered the tools and wiped his sweaty forehead with the sleeve of his flannel. It may only be the beginning of June, but the sun was well over the horizon by 6 o'clock in the morning. Today was going to be a hot one.

"Hungry?" Logan called to Mike, who was loading up his quad.

"What do you think?"

"Flatlands in a half hour?" Logan suggested.

Mike straddled and started the quad in one smooth, well-practiced motion. "See you there." And with a wave, he took off.

As if on cue, Logan's stomach let out a loud growl. He hopped into his side-by-side and followed Mike's tracks left by the early morning dew. The five-minute drive back to the ranch house allowed Logan a moment to admire the view of his property. He loved his five hundred acre cattle ranch just outside of Sethburn, Saskatchewan. He had worked almost a decade at making this parcel of land a place he could call home. Moving here at the age of sixteen with just his father and hardly any ranching experience was overwhelming. But Lincoln and Logan Fraser had made a great team when faced all kinds of adversity—which was what sent them on their way to Sethburn in the first place.

Logan crested the small hill and in the distance, his ranch house came into view. Just a few hundred feet behind it was the original home of the property, which was now occupied by his father on the top floor, while Mike had the basement to himself. Two years ago, Logan had put the finishing touches on the humbly sized, two-bedroom log house he had built for himself. Lincoln had understood that once he signed over the property to his son, Logan would want his own residence, so the two had started the project four years ago. It took a while to build because the two of them could fit in only a few hours to build between the daily workings of the ranch.

Last year, when Lincoln had claimed he was old enough—at a mere sixty years of age—for semi-retirement, Logan brought on Mike as a ranch hand. The interview process had been an easy one. Logan posted a want ad in the 'Sethburn Times', the weekly paper, and one on an online classifieds page. Few young men wanted to move to a small town like Sethburn, so from the three men who had applied, Mike had been an easy choice. He had family in the area, which Logan had yet to meet in last fourteen months, and he had experience with cattle.

Mike mostly stuck to himself in Lincoln's basement, only sur-facing occasionally for food, but was sociable enough to join the guys once in a while for breakfast at the diner when he didn't travel home—wherever that was—on the weekends. It was obvious Mike didn't like sharing much about himself, so Logan never pressed for more information. If he pulled his weight around the ranch, it didn't matter much to Logan what was going on with his ranch hand's personal life. If Logan had to guess based on a few moments of weakness and some comments said under his breath, Mike had woman problems. So did Logan. And since Logan hated talking about his own, he never brought it up with Mike.

Logan pulled in next to his own back entrance and parked the side-by-side. One thing he made sure of when building his own home was a laundry room large enough to leave all of his muddy, manure covered gear in after a long day on the ranch. He striped his wet boots off and placed them on a rubber mat before tossing his jacket near the closet on the opposite side of the room. He'd hang it up some time—right now, he wanted a hot shower to shake off this morning's activities and follow that with a big breakfast with an even bigger cup of coffee from the diner.

After throwing on a pair of dry Levis, a t-shirt, and a Blue Jays hat, Logan went back to the boot room to find his favorite pair of worn out sneakers. He shoved his wet jacket out of the way and pushed open the closet door. He was sure he had tossed them in there after last time he wore them. He took one look at the pile of jackets, coveralls, and boots on the floor of the closet then compared it to the empty hangers that hung untouched above the mess. Then he decided to do something about the mess over the weekend, but for now, the faster he dug, the faster he would be digging into a stack of pancakes.

After two minutes, Logan found both shoes at the bottom of the pile. He stood too quickly and bumped his head on the lowest shelf. Dusty boxes, a set of bolt cutters, a hammer, and a screwdriver fell onto the already large heap. The box tipped and out spilled papers photographs, and other mementos all over the floor. Not wasting more time, Logan reached down to gather only the most obvious tripping hazards that blocked his path to the door. He pushed the photographs and papers together, but the object that ended up on top of the pile left him dropping them right where they had spilled.

It was the first 4-H award Logan earned when he was just fourteen—the Leadership Award. His mother decided to get him more involved in the community outside of Calgary that fall. Logan and four other boys were given the task of making a business plan for a beginner livestock farm that would start out with fifteen cows, one bull, five pigs, and two horses. The plan had to sustain the farm for three years. Logan agreed to head up the project, and their presentation was flawless after months of hard work. That was when Logan decided he wanted to be a rancher. His mother had been so proud of their whole team when the winners were announced. That had been a good day.

His rush to leave was momentarily forgotten, and the familiar harbored anger rose to the surface as Logan stared at the clunky medal. Logan reached for the papers a second time and threw the entire stack back into the box without a second glance at the award when he tossed that in too. He shoved his sneakers on, scooped up the box, and bee-lined it outside to the dumpster. With no regard for the rest of its contents, Logan pitched the entire box inside releasing the heavy lid to slam down on top of it. From across the yard, Lincoln gave Logan a curious look and a half-hearted wave. He didn't return the gesture.

It was time for pancakes.

MIKE beat him to Flatlands and snagged their favorite booth near the back. Logan slipped into the opposite side of the booth already signaling Earl, the owner who could always be found behind the counter, for a coffee. This was Logan's favourite place to eat. It served breakfast from dawn until dusk, and the menu had been the same since Earl had opened its doors decades earlier, as had the orange and lime green décor. It was predictable and reliable, unlike any woman.

Carmen, their waitress, sashayed up to the table with a butler in one hand and a few mugs in the other. She filled each mug with practiced skill while at the same time placing their cutlery on either side of the table.

"Mornin', fellas. The usual?" she winked at Logan, even though she addressed them both.

Carmen had had a crush on Logan as long as he could remember. In fact, a year ago, Earl had informed him she'd be the waitress for the back section of tables for the foreseeable future—'as per her request'. Logan didn't mind, since it meant great service every time he sat down.

Mike, even though he was a diligent regular, perused the menu every visit with no exception to this morning. He spoke up with his eyes still on the menu, "Actually, Carmen, I'll have the omelet this morning. No mushrooms."

Carmen cocked a hip. "Mike, that's the same thing you've ordered the last three times you've been here. It's your new usual."

Mike shrugged off her sass. "Then the usual, please."

She turned to Logan. "You, sugar?"

Logan smiled at their exchange. "The usual."

"Stack 'a six with extra butter and extra bacon," she confirmed. "Earl's thinkin' about renaming it 'the Logan.'" She snatched the menu from Mike and trotted off with a smirk.

Logan stabbed his fork into a creamer and squirted the contents into his mug. "Plans this weekend? Thinking of hitting up the gun range. You in?" he asked Mike.

"Nah. Goin' home."

Logan, again, didn't ask any further questions. He guessed that Mike's 'home' was close by, probably no more than a few hours' drive. He was just glad Mike had family he cared enough about to want to spend time with. Maybe envious too, not that he would admit it.

"I assumed you would have a date for tonight by now," Mike added.

Logan snorted derisively. "Oh yeah? With who?"

"Carmen."

Logan contemplated it. He had never asked her on a date before—she was one of the few in Sethburn he hadn't been out with yet. It used to be that he always worried it would make things awkward whenever he came to the diner, because Logan never dated a woman more than a few times. But since he had dated another waitress, Sheila, once or twice, what did it matter? He liked their company to pass the time, but women were never to be trusted. Today, he considered it because, frankly, that worthless 4-H medal he found in his house this morning had shook him up more than he cared to admit. What better way to take his mind off of it?

"Not a bad idea."

Their breakfast was delivered a few minutes later. Carmen lingered at the table waiting for them to take a bit so she could ask Logan how he liked it. It made for an easy transition into asking her out.

"Carmen, I bet these pancakes are a close second to the new pizza joint in Shell Lake."

She swatted his arm playfully. "Hey, buster, you know Earl's got the best food north 'a Saskatoon."

"Want to test it out with me tonight? You know, just to be sure." He flashed her his charming grin.

Her eyes grew large as she gasped in air before choking on the big breath. Mike held in his laughter and looked away to avoid another embarrassing situation, while Logan watched her coughing play out to make sure she was actually okay. Once she had control of her breathing again, she asked, "You mean it?"

"'Course."

With stars in her eyes, she replied, "Then yes."

"Pick you up at six."

As Carmen floated away, Mike said, "You know I was only kidding about asking her out, right?"

"I wasn't," Logan said more forcefully than intended.

The men ate their breakfast in silence, and Mike left for the ranch while chewing his last bite. He told Logan he wanted to get on the road as soon as he could. As Mike slid out of the booth, Drake Hemming slid in.

"Morning," said Logan's best friend of the past decade.

Logan returned the greeting and finished off his coffee in one gulp. Drake had been the first guy to select him for a game of dodge ball in a schoolyard pick back in tenth grade. The two had been inseparable ever since. Well, that's not quite true. Even as teenager, Drake always seemed to have his neighbour, Anna, stealing his time now and again. By graduation, Logan was surprised those two didn't have a wedding in the works, but Anna's decision to leave Sethburn—and everyone in it—to pursue a university degree hours away had shocked everyone, including Logan. Not that he told anyone, but Logan hadn't minded the extra time it gave him with his best friend. Last summer, however, Anna came back to Sethburn to help her sister, Sophie, start up a matchmaking company. Drake was quick to try to rekindle their romance, but Anna had dug in her heels. It had taken a few months of convincing, but Drake and Anna were engaged by Christmas. Logan would be the best man at the ceremony that was just two months away.

Anna and Drake were two of his closest friends, and he was happy to see them getting married and planning a future together. It didn't mean he, himself was all for marriage though. Creating a family and making it stick was tricky business. A business he wanted no part of.

Drake gestured across the diner for refill. "Plans this weekend?"

It didn't take Carmen more than five seconds to be at their table with a full butler. Logan looked up at her as she filled both mugs and winked. "Yeah, some."

She giggled as she left.

Drake sighed. "Really, man? Carmen?"

Logan shrugged.

"You know, it doesn't have to be like that. Dating someone can last more than a few hours if you put some effort into it."

Logan hated when Drake lectured him about his dating life. He understood that what Drake and Anna had was a rarity. And that kind of relationship just wasn't in the cards for him.

"Drake, I've heard it from you before. I'm not meant for a life like yours. Let's leave it at that."

Drake raised his hands in mock surrender. "Whatever you say. Just trying to help you be as happy as I am."

Logan saluted him with his mug. "Thanks, anyway."

Two

Sophie Rempel spun the lid onto her travel mug and gathered her purse. She didn't see the point in locking up, especially in a town as small as Sethburn, but her big city sister insisted that their door above the Coleman's garage was to be locked at all times. She twisted the key in the deadbolt and made her way downstairs to her car. The suite was a little less than seven hundred square feet. Two bedrooms, a studio kitchen, which was fine since their mother insisted on at least three family dinners a week that she came home with leftovers from, an area barely large enough for a love seat and a small television, and the tiniest bathroom known to mankind. But it suited her and Anna just fine once they agreed on a bathroom schedule.

Last fall, when her matchmaking business Match 'Em Up was established, Sophie decided to make another change—move out of her parents' house. It had taken one afternoon of perusing the classifieds, meeting up with the Colemans who were long time family friends, and a signature on a two-page lease agreement to make that change. After thrift store shopping and a trip into Saskatoon for the rest, the suite was furnished. Just weeks after the move, Anna came back to Sethburn permanently, much to Sophie's delight. In the last year, their sisterly relationship had gone from non-existent with a few short, curt calls a year to a deeply rooted friendship that could withstand whatever life was going to throw at them. Not only were they roommates now, they were truly best friends.

Sophie parked at the back entrance of her office and went inside to start her day. Match 'Em Up started out as a daydream Sophie would relive during her dull afternoons working at Sethburn's only post office. In a conservative Christian town like Sethburn, matchmaking was unheard of. It was an idea that was too 'out there' for the town's comfort zone. But bored with her monotonous life of working nine to five, living with her parents, and hanging out at the diner with the same friends every weekend, Sophie took her career into her own hands.

Sethburn, however, along with several other small towns in the area, had embraced the idea of matchmaking with little convincing. It had been a shock to everyone, especially Sophie. Now, not even a year in, her business was thriving. She had people all over northern Saskatchewan signing up. Her clientele base was well over five hundred and growing.

Stepping from the back room into the front office, Sophie studied her 'match wall'. It had been Anna's idea to document successful relationships started at Match 'Em Up with a commemorative photo wall. So far, only three portraits hung there. One, a wedding photo of the Keller couple. Rick was a forty-year-old school principal who invested all of his thirties into bettering the lives of students at his school leaving no time for a social life. Peggy was a thirty-seven year old grocery store manager who moved from Winnipeg two years ago. Her mother had Parkinson's disease; so for much of her life, Peggy had spent taking care of her mother full time. The small town life had always appealed to her, so a year after her mother had passed away, she made the move to Sethburn.

Their courtship had been a whirlwind and a pleasure for Sophie to watch. Within six weeks of Sophie setting them up on a first date at the local golf course—a hobby both of them shared—they became engaged. Sophie had been a bridesmaid at their New Year's wedding.

The other two photos were from engagement sessions. Andrew and Leah became engaged shortly after Andrew taught Leah how to operator a tractor. She had said, "That was it for me! A handsome man and some heavy machinery—what more could a girl ask for?"

Reynold and Rachael's photograph hung next to Andrew and Leah's. They were probably her most favourite couple she had matched so far. Both had been matched with three other people before they went on their first date. Their age had been the only thing they had in common with Reynold being a bush pilot while Rachael spent her days teaching ballet to children. Reynold was six foot five with a beard that could rival any lumberjack's, and Rachael was petite at five-two with a flaming-red hairstyle that needed a root touch up every three weeks. One date at the town's park for a picnic and they knew.

She stowed her purse in the filing cabinet adjacent to her desk and booted up her computer. Every morning before anything else, Sophie checked her email for follow-ups on the previous night's matchups. It was her policy that after the first date, each client would send her a quick email letting her know the success—or failure—of the date. That way she knew if both clients were satisfied and ready for a second date, or in some cases, if the feelings of each client were not reciprocated, Sophie can check for a new match.

With only one matchup from last night, two new client emails were waiting in her inbox.

Josh B: *I had a great time with Sarah last night. Even though the ice cream place didn't have mint chocolate chip, we still managed to have a great time. We already planned date #2! You're the best J*

Sarah W: *Sophie, you were right! It wasn't too soon since my last break up to get back out there. Josh is great—kept me laughing all night. We're seeing each other again on Saturday!*

Sophie smiled at this couple's success and sent off a reply to each of them encouraging them to contact her with any questions about date ideas in and around the area. She also told them their information would be kept on file for a minimum of three months, and she would contact them again in one month to ask about the progress.

Reaching for the stack of new applications she had received over the course of a week, Sophie began inputting each client's new data into her software program that developed the matches. It was a detailed application questioning each client about things like their faith, childhood, criminal records, health history, parenting preferences, habits, and hobbies, among other things.

This program often made her wonder who her own matches would be. She had yet to become brave enough to match her own information with the list of clientele. It would be inappropriate for her to date a client anyway. Over the years, men have showed interest in her from time to time, but hardly any men had ever piqued her interest. She'd been on a few dates, but usually the courtship would last a few dates at most. She had only one boyfriend in the twenty-six years she'd been alive, and Edward had caught her eye on the playground when she was in fourth grade. They had dated on and off for a week, he'd been her first kiss under the monkey bars, but much to her nine-year-old heart's dismay, they weren't meant to last. The next Monday at school, she caught him pulling Suzy's pigtails by the swing set. And that was that.

In high school, there had been one boy in particular that expressed interest in pursuing her. He had asked her out a total of nine times in the span of a single semester. He had persistence; she'd give him that. But he had been a bad boy back then—breaking dress code rules with his ever present ball cap, skipping home room to drip honey all over the girls' washrooms, and even parking his rusty pick-up truck in the principal's spot and then timed it from the first bell to when Mr. Wright came and found him. Today, he still had a reputation, but now it had more to do with the ladies of Sethburn than childish pranks. As a teen, Sophie had been more interested in any Dee Henderson novel than dating a city boy. Or at least, Sophie had assumed he was one because he'd moved from Calgary to Sethburn. But now, Logan was one of her good friends. He was the best friend with her soon to be brother-in-law, which meant she saw him quite frequently. Drake often roped him into helping her out with setting up Match 'Em Up's monthly mixers. He was helpful and kind, but he was known for his charm, which he often used to get his way around Sethburn, whether with the ladies or anything else. Graduation was the last time he had asked her out, and she guessed he had finally taken no as an answer.

Now though, she wasn't so sure she would be quick to decline his offer. Even though his reputation was well known, Sophie wondered if it would be worth her time to get to know him a little better. She quickly pushed the thought aside to continue inputting new applications. She had a business to focus on.

The bell on the door chimed, and Sophie looked up to see Anna come into her office juggling a coffee tray, a to-go bag of what looked like goodies from Flatlands, and a heavy portfolio. Which meant only one thing—wedding talk.

So far, as maid of honour, Sophie had assisted with choosing the dress, booking a venue, making invitations, meeting the photographer, tasting cakes—her favourite activity thus far, arranging the seating plan, and planning the surprise bridal shower with their mother, Rita. She figured that by the time she was going to be a bride, planning would be a breeze.

Sophie reached for the coffee tray and food before it all came tumbling down.

"I'm hoping one of these is a double-double for me?"

Anna shrugged out of her jacket and hung it on the stylish rack by the door before taking a seat on one of the leather chairs Sophie had in her meeting area. "Well, since I crashed your morning and distracted you from a business that pays your rent, yes, I brought you a peace offering."

Sophie put the tray on the coffee table, took her coffee out, and sat down across from Anna. "What's in the bag?" she asked even though her nose and stomach had already determined it was Earl's famous cherry strudels.

Anna smirked. "A bribe."

Sophie had a sneaking suspicion that another maid of honour favour was about to be cashed in. "For?"

"I may or may not be wanting to change the colour of your dress."

Sophie groaned. This would be the third time Anna had changed her mind about the bridal party wardrobe. She had already reordered the best man's suit changing it from black to charcoal and changed the bridesmaid's dress from floor length to tea length. Last Sophie knew her dress was going to be teal. "To what colour? My pale skin doesn't compliment much," she joked.

Anna took a long pull of her coffee. "Maybe coral," she said barely above a whisper.

But Sophie heard it loud and clear. Everyone who knew her well knew that Sophie was not a fan of pink. Like, at all. Coral definitely fell under the pink umbrella. Sophie took a moment while kindly glaring at her sister to evaluate the pros and cons. It was an easy decision. Anna was her sister and best friend, and Sophie wanted her to have the wedding she wished for, nothing less. If that meant wearing a coral, tea length, chiffon brides-maid's dress then that was what she would wear.

"Then coral it is."

"Really?" Anna practically came out of her seat.

"Absolutely. But as the maid of honour, I must remind you that your wedding is approaching at warp speed, and I would much rather have a coral dress to wear than nothing at all. So if you wouldn't mind expediting the shipping on that, I would greatly appreciate it."

Anna already had her cell phone out. It was obvious Anna had faith Sophie wouldn't balk the new colour, since the page was ready for Anna to hit 'Order'.

"Done and done. You may have a strudel now."

Sophie laughed and dug a strudel from the bag for each of them. She might as well embrace the rewards of being a compla-cent maid of honour.

"Have you gotten all your shower gifts put away at Drake's yet?" Sophie asked.

The bridal shower had been last weekend. Sophie and Rita had hosted it in the church's multipurpose room. It was a room large enough for forty ladies, a small kitchen, and a few tables for the buffet. The event had been a great success leaving Anna with an entire truck box full of early wedding gifts. Ladies from the church, all over Sethburn, and several of Sophie's clients from around the area who had met Anna through Match 'Em Up had been in attendance. Sophie had even managed to host the Sunday afternoon without so much as a cheesy wedding word scramble game or toilet paper dress fashion show.

It was another afternoon that confirmed that Sethburn was truly one of the best places on the planet. The hospitality and fun had by all the ladies had been contagious, and everyone left with a smile. Anna had been overwhelmed by the support, and that evening, both Drake and Sophie had to keep reminding Anna that the gifts that now took up Drake's entire dining room were, indeed, all of theirs.

"Sure did," Anna answered, "It meant packing up a few of his parents' things, but we managed to get everything stored away." Drake's parents had died several years ago, and Drake had taken over their farmhouse.

"That must have been hard for him," Sophie said.

Anna relaxed into the chair. "Actually, he said it was nice packing away some of their things. He told me it made him more excited to start our new life together in that house. We are making it our own, starting with new things. I can't wait to move in."

Sophie was sad to see her roommate go, but the excitement about the wedding and her sister's happiness far outweighed Anna moving out after the wedding.

The phone rang reminding them that Sophie still had a business to run even if it was more fun to sit in cozy chairs and chat away the day. It was Mona from Shell Lake's community hall wanting to confirm the booking for the next mixer. After Sophie had verified the hall rental, she sat back in her office chair and looked to Anna.

"We'd better get to work, Sis. I've got a mixer to plan."

Match 'Em Up held a monthly mixer for all of Sophie's clients along with anyone who RSVP'd with an interest in signing up with the company. It was a great way to spread word of mouth about her business and an even better way for her clients to give her feedback on any potential matches they may have met. The evening usually started with casual mingling over appetizers and punch. Alcohol was never allowed at Sophie's events. She ran a Christian organization, and she was not going to be basing her success on an out of hand client. Anyone who attended the mixers would be making connections while sober. The night ended with music and a dance floor.

Anna and Sophie spent the next hour side by side making arrangements with caterers, florists, and the live band Sophie had hired. It would be the first mixer with live music, and she was hoping that would draw a larger crowd. But with a larger crowd came more food and decorations, which meant they would be recruiting help.

"I know just who to call," Anna said.

"Oh, Anna, I always feel bad for asking Drake and Logan. We should think of someone else this time," Sophie whined.

"Who says I'll just be asking Drake and Logan? I say it's high time for Logan to bring his ranch hand along too. Mike, I think. Three big, strong guys will have that party set up in no time."

"So we convince them it'll be more fun with another friend?"

"Sophie, I don't have to do much convincing. We're engaged and want to spend every minute together, remember? Helping you out is practically 'date night' for us," Anna said with a smile.

"And the other two? Just out of the goodness of their hearts?"

"Mike probably, yes. But we both know Logan will stick around and enjoy himself. Single ladies and all."

Sophie almost blushed as her sister's comment reminded her of her earlier thoughts about the man in question. She was right though; Logan had helped before and was known for sticking around to enjoy the party. However, he had yet to become a real client of hers. He had reluctantly filled out an application last year at her first mixer because she had practically begged everyone, but when she followed up with him a few weeks later, he wanted nothing to do with being matched up.

"This time Logan can only stay if he agrees to be matched up. If he wants to stick around, he has to play by the rules."

Anna laughed. "Good thinking. But Sophie?"

"Yeah?"

"Good luck with that."

Three

Logan cruised down the narrow highway glad he turned on the radio before picking up Carmen. He wasn't much for excessive small talk, and since he wasn't sure how much they would have to talk about in the first place, he opted for listening to his favourite country music station on the half hour drive to Shell Lake's pizzeria. He glanced over at her a few times on the way to make sure she enjoyed the music. She tapped her knee to the beat during a few songs, so Logan kept it tuned to country.

After parking in front of the pizzeria, Logan leapt out to open the passenger door for Carmen. As she climbed out of his truck, she landed then teetered on the extremely high, skinny heel of her sandal. They were the most impractical footwear Logan had ever laid eyes on. At the diner, he could remember Carmen only ever sporting comfortable looking white sneakers, and now as he came to think of it, he liked her better that way. It seemed to him that dates would be more fun when both participants were able to easily walk to and from a restaurant without balancing their body weight on a surface the size of a dime.

But to each his own, he decided. He wouldn't let it ruin his evening with a good pizza and a pretty girl.

Logan held open the door letting her go first into the restaurant. She chose a booth by the window, and they both ordered a Pepsi to drink.

Logan read over the laminated menu that had been sandwiched between the salt and pepper shakers. "Drake and I have been here once. The Hawaiian pizza is good, but the Meat Lovers is even better. Do you want to split one? Half what you want, half what I want?"

Carmen spied the menu and flared her nostrils in distaste. "Actually, I'm going to stick with a salad."

Logan frowned. He had told her the restaurant choice earlier, and she hadn't mentioned that she didn't like pizza.

"Would you rather go somewhere else?" he asked.

Carmen answered quickly, "No, no. Just watchin' my figure is all. Any place across from you is just fine with me." She batted her eyelashes at him.

He gave her a fake smile in return. Logan didn't know why women refused to enjoy their meals. He wasn't asking them to eat in excess, he just wanted to them to at least enjoy the taste of it. Few people would choose watery lettuce over a cheesy pizza, and if he had to guess, Carmen probably wished she chose the latter.

A memory of last week popped into his mind. Drake, Anna, her sister, Sophie, and himself all went to Flatlands for a late breakfast last Saturday. Anna challenged Sophie to a pancake eating competition—who could eat the most in five minutes. Sophie had annihilated her sister eating five dinner plate sized pancakes in five minutes. Anna had barely started her third by the time was up. He had been impressed and left wondering if he could even beat Sophie at the same challenge. It had been fun to watch that was for sure.

While waiting for their meals, Logan steered the conversation away from their food choices. He didn't know much about Carmen except that she worked at Flatlands.

"So Carmen, what do you do in your free time?" he asked.

She leaned her elbows on the table and folded her arms under her chin before speaking. "Well, Logan, I just *love* to babysit my nephew. He's two now—it's such a fun age. You know, I got him this little lasso for his birthday, and he flings that thing around like a real rancher." She reached out her hand and grabbed ahold of Logan's arm. "I'll bet he'll be as good as you in no time."

He carefully pried her grip from his bicep and replaced her hand to her side of the table. "Contrary to popular belief, not all ranchers can lasso a steer. I have never even tried, actually."

Carmen gave a little pout then batted her eyelashes. "I've watched Tommy a few times—maybe I can teach you."

Logan internally rolled his eyes at her overt flirting tactics. He had no desire to learn to lasso, and even if he did, he doubted he would call up Carmen to show him. In fact, he was sure that he wouldn't. "Thanks for the offer," he said, "I'll keep you in mind next time I rope some cattle."

She sipped her drink before asking, "And you, Logan? What happens in your free time?"

Logan sat back in the comfortable booth. "When I'm not out with pretty girls like you, I'm working on little projects around the ranch. There's always something to do."

She giggled at his compliment. "I saw you in the paper last month. You know, with that cute little calf all cuddled up nice on your lap. You were bottle-feeding her, and it was like she was looking at you like you held the moon and the stars. It was just absolutely the sweetest thing I've ever seen."

Logan groaned. He made Pete, the reporter, promise he'd leave the picture out of the article, but no such luck. The Friday after Pete made the visit to the ranch, the story was published along with the picture. On the front cover—'Local Rancher With Soft Heart For Herd'. The calf had been a triplet, and her mother couldn't support all three babies, so this one had been left out. Logan had done what any rancher would do. He bottle-fed that calf until she was able to eat on her own, and now, she was a troublemaker. Number eight-four—the one he rescued from the fence just that morning.

"Glad you enjoyed it. I asked him not to run the picture, and then I ended up on the cover." He shrugged. There wasn't much he could do about it now.

"Well, you looked as handsome as ever." She gave him a playful swat on the arm.

Thankfully, their food arrived, and Logan escaped the awkward conversation. Apparently, it didn't take long to throw together a pizza and a salad.

He almost felt bad eating his cheesy, delicious pizza in front of a woman who clearing wasn't enjoying her salad as much as she enjoyed watching the cheese drip from his chin, but he was able to ignore any sense of guilt by the time he bit into his third slice.

When the waitress came to clear off their plates, Carmen was particularly interested in the dessert menu. Logan guessed she was probably still hungry. She ordered her own helping of Mud Pie Madness—the menu specifically explained that it was best to share because it was so huge.

Her words were, "I'll take home whatever is left over. My nephew just loves chocolate."

She ate every last bite.

On the drive back to Sethburn, Logan wasn't so lucky with the radio. She shut it off almost immediately.

"So tell me about your fancy new log home. I've seen it driving by, and it looks fabulous," Carmen said.

Logan shrugged—it seemed to be his gesture of the evening. "I like it. It took my dad and I forever to get that thing finished, but I was picky. Everything was built just the way I like it."

"How big is it?"

"Two bedrooms, two bathrooms, and a common area for the kitchen, dining room, and living room."

She clasped her hands together in excitement. "Wow! So plenty of room for a family. That's so great."

Logan risked a glance to her side of his truck. She looked perfectly wistful about the possibility that one day soon it would be her occupying his home. Whereas, an hour into the date, he was certain his future would not include Carmen. And as far as he knew, his future wouldn't involve anyone but his father and his friends.

No woman was worth risking a repeat of his childhood.

AFTER dropping Carmen off and politely declining a second date—well, as politely as he could while he pried her hand off of his bicep, Logan started for home. His house was ten kilometers north of Sethburn giving him the feel of secluded living while still being close to necessities. He pulled over at the rural mailboxes just outside of town to pick up the ranch's mail. His, Lincoln's, and Mike's mail all came to the same box making it easier for picking up.

Once back in the truck, he sifted through the pile sorting each person's as he went. Mostly bills for him along with Sethburn's newspaper and Cabela's hunting catalog. Mike's pile was small as usual—a phone bill, a Reader's Digest, and one bright blue envelope with crayon drawings of hockey sticks all over it. At least, Logan guessed it was hockey sticks.

As Logan got to the bottom of the stack, a thick magazine got his attention. He pulled it out and took a closer look. It was a copy of *Nashville Music Quarterly*. Before he allowed his anger to take over, Logan double-checked the address just to make sure it was really his father who ordered the magazine. Sure enough, Lincoln Fraser had purchased this copy. It took his full restraint to not rip the magazine to shreds. Just as he was about to chuck it onto his passenger seat, he noticed the words on the cover. And it almost stopped his heart.

Stacy-Lynn Fraser Takes Home Eighth ACMA!

With what little control Logan had left, he drove the rest of the way to the ranch. He pulled up and parked at his father's house and grabbed the stacks of mail. He took the steps two at a time to the front door and rushed in without knocking.

He found Lincoln laid back in his usual recliner watching pre-season CFL highlights.

"You've got to be kidding me." Logan threw the magazine into his father's lap.

Lincoln stared at his lap for several moments without making a sound.

"You going to explain yourself?" Logan asked.

Finally, Lincoln replied, "Son, you know I keep tabs occasionally."

Logan did know it. Two years ago, he found a newspaper clipping from the Calgary Post bragging about their hometown girl who made it to the biggest stage in country music. Just six months ago, Lincoln had left his email open on the ranch's office computer, and Logan had found quite a lengthy message from her asking how calving season was going, how the ranch hand was working out, how her son was doing. Logan had lost it then and tried to drag a promise from Lincoln that he would cut off all contact to her. Lincoln had never succumbed to his son's pressure.

"I thought we talked about this, Dad."

Lincoln sat up in his chair and looked Logan in the eye. He knew that look—it was one that meant business.

"No, son, *you* talked about it. And I never promised you a thing. She was the biggest part of my life. She's my *wife*. I cared deeply for her then, and I care deeply for her now. Nothing, not even her leaving or your lectures and anger, will change that."

Logan lowered himself to the couch across from Lincoln. "You can't mean that," he whispered.

"I mean every word," Lincoln lifted the magazine showing Logan the cover, "And I want to know about her accomplishments. I want to know that she didn't do it all for nothing."

Logan seethed. "You want to know if abandoning her husband and son, the two people that should matter most, above everything else, wasn't all for nothing?"

"Look at me, Logan."

He complied.

"I want to know that she's happy."

Logan couldn't believe his father's words. How could the man in front of him still care for a woman who tore their world apart, who left them to chase fame?

"I just don't get it, Dad."

A long, silent moment passed then Lincoln stood and headed for the kitchen. "I want to show you something. Maybe it'll help you understand where I'm coming from."

He came back with a small devotional book and passed it to Logan. "Open today's page," he asked.

Logan did. He wasn't much for daily devotions or regular church attendance after what happened to his family a decade ago. But because his dad, the man he most respected for making a life for both of them after a tragedy, asked him to, he read the verse aloud. "Love keeps no record of wrongs."

"It's my favourite verse—1 Corinthians 13:5. Logan, you need to get your head around the fact that I still love your mother, and yeah, I was pretty angry when she left. But look there," he pointed to the small book, "If I love her it's pretty tough to carry around a list of her mistakes."

Even though it was easy to hold onto the anger he harbored for his mother, Logan struggled to stay angry with his father. The man sitting across from him was still in love with a woman who didn't love him back, and that made it pretty difficult to be mad about. Instead, he felt sad for the man.

Logan let out a long sigh and handed the devotional back. "I might not understand why you still love Mom, but I get that you want to keep tabs."

"Thank you, son. That means a whole lot."

Both men seemed finished with the conversation for now. If too many more feelings were exposed the room might to start to smell like flowers or something. They both sat back in their respective chairs and tuned in to the day's sports highlights.

During the commercial break, Lincoln retrieved two cans of Pepsi from the refrigerator and tossed one to Logan.

"How was the date, by the way? Mike said you were going out," Lincoln asked him.

Logan relived the evening in his mind for a few seconds before replying, "Meh."

Lincoln laughed out loud. "She's not the one, eh?"

Logan was well aware of the sarcasm from his dad, but he shrugged it off.

"You know my policy," he said.

Four

Logan's left arm was slung over his steering wheel gently guiding the truck down the highway towards his destination. His right hand was finding his favourite country radio station, and his eyes hid behind his aviators scanning the roadway and ditches for traffic and wildlife. Tonight he and Drake were headed to Shell Lake's community hall—they had been recruited for their muscles to transport and set up the heavy items for tonight's Match 'Em Up mixer. Logan's window was rolled all the way down because it was the hottest day Sethburn had so far this June, but the passenger window stayed closed.

"I don't want to wreck my hair," Drake said.

"Since when are you into vanity?" Logan laughed and remembered his own plaid button down, jeans, and ball cap.

Drake looked over sheepishly. "Since Anna did my hair earlier when I stopped by to pick up the stuff for tonight's mixer."

Logan roared. "I hate to tell you this, bud, but it looks the same as it does every other day."

This time Drake smiled back. "I know."

Logan readjusted his ball cap, tugging it low on his head so it wouldn't blow off from the wind in the cab. "Glad I don't have a girl who does my hair."

"You do," Drake added, "Her name is Glenda, and she has owned the barbershop for over thirty years. I believe you have a standing appointment on the first Monday of every month."

Logan snorted. "You know what I mean."

"Yeah, but it's more fun if I tease you about Glenda."

"What's going to happen for the wedding or the bachelor party? Surely, she won't let you out of the house with your regular, yet strikingly the same, hairstyle. You would definitely be exposed to mockery and ridicule—especially from your best man. I'm sure he'd really stick it to ya," Logan explained with sarcasm.

"Ha-ha. But speaking of bachelor parties, Anna wants to do a joint one. You know, more like an engagement party just closer to the wedding," Drake said.

"And you're going to go along with it, aren't you? Are you saying you love Anna more than me?" Logan asked with mock surprise.

"Absolutely," Drake said.

Logan sighed. He wondered how it would feel to love a woman that much. "Now you're really just sucking the fun out of it. We were going to have an awesome day being guys—nine holes, paintball, and skeet shooting. Then finish off the night with the biggest, juiciest rack of ribs you have ever laid eyes on." Logan flicked on his signal light to turn towards the hall that was just a few blocks down. "It's huge, believe me. It's currently taking up half my deep freeze."

Logan pulled into a parking space right by the entrance just as Anna walked outside. Drake whistled and drummed his fingers on the door handle. "That does sound good. Maybe we can fit that all in before the other thing."

"What other thing?" Anna said through Logan's open window.

Logan spoke up before Drake had a chance. "We thought of a better party that'll happen before your lame joint party."

Anna grinned at Logan's playfulness. "Let me guess, it involves a sporting activity and a gun."

Both men burst out laughing. "You got it, babe," Drake said.

"Well," Anna said turning back towards the hall, "you boys should put the party planning aside and start unloading this truck."

It took a while to get everything inside, and it took even longer to set up and move tables around as Sophie and Anna deliberating several spots for each one. Logan stayed patient as long as he could, but left to help the band set up the stage when he got tired of the girls deciding if the tables should border the dance floor or not. He promised to come back once they finally made a decision.

BY eight o'clock that night the hall was buzzing with noise and excitement. Logan had been to a few of Sophie's mixers, and none of them had ever been this well attended. He liked to mingle at these events—sometimes, he even get a few phone numbers without Sophie noticing, but he usually tried to sneak out as soon as the dance began. Earlier, Sophie had asked if he could stay until the end to help take down the tables and chairs. With her fancy hair, pretty dress, and polite manners, he couldn't say no.

He sipped his punch as he scanned the room. There had to be at least forty women and just as many men milling around the buffet and the dance floor. The women were all shapes and sizes—just the way he liked them, but his gaze kept landing on the evening's host. Sophie hustled around the room restocking appetizers, checking on the band, and answering everyone's questions about her business all while staying calm and collected. She did it with such confidence in her summer dress and flip-flops. Logan decided he would change his usual policy and dance with her before the night was over.

Just then, he spotted Carmen coming his way, leaving no time for him to come up with an escape route. He checked the vicinity to ensure that it was, indeed, him that she was aiming for, and sure enough, the closest person to him stood a good ten feet away. She stopped with barely a foot of space between them.

"Fancy meeting you here," she said with a wink.

He tipped his head to her yet avoided eye contact. Sophie disappeared from the spot near the buffet he just saw her at, so he took stock of the hall once again. It was still weird seeing Carmen without her waitress uniform and white sneakers and add in the awkwardness from their date, Logan really wanted to avoid this whole situation.

Carmen reached out and smoothed his collar down even though it didn't need it. "You know, I had a great time last night," she whispered.

Logan hated these situations, and again, he found himself questioning why he kept putting himself in them. If he just withstood another quiet night at home instead of listening to her make their family plans over salad and pizza, he wouldn't have to hurt her feelings now.

He looked down at her. "Look, Carmen—"

Anguished washed over her features. "Are you breaking up with me?" she asked too loudly.

People at the closest tables looked over at them, and Logan tried to politely wave them off while coming up with an idea for damage control.

"Sweetheart, we went on one date. That hardly makes us a couple."

A tear slid down her cheek taking mascara with it. "My friends said this would happen. B-but I thought we had s-something special, Logan," she sputtered.

Now Logan was getting frustrated. Why did women do this? One minute they say whatever they think he wants to hear, and the next they're blowing a pizza date way out of proportion, making it the magnitude of matrimony.

"I don't know what your friends said, but Carmen, we shared a meal and some conversation. I'm not going to commit to anything."

She swiped at her tears smearing makeup everywhere, then sniffed good and loud before asking, "Is there s-something wrong with me?"

Here we go. "No, there's nothing wrong with you."

"Then w-why don't you like me?"

People were staring. This needed to end now. Logan gently grasped her elbow and ushered her towards the exit. He leaned down to whisper, "I like you just fine. I think we could be good friends."

Once out the door, she spun around, and he lost his hold on her arm. He knew what was coming next—the anger phase. She stabbed her finger into his chest. "But you don't *like me* like me. This is exactly what they said would happen—you'd brush me off after one date like I was garbage on the curb. All I wanted was to get to know you, Logan. I just wanted a chance, you know. I deserve," she drilled her finger into him, "a chance."

Then she began to sob, as in full dry heave, bent over sob. And finally the closure phase. Logan stroked her back until she got ahold of herself.

"Let me tell you something, Carmen. You deserve better than me. I'm a pretty messed up guy. So why don't you march back into that hall and find your Mr. Right." He hoped that sounded good. He'd do anything to make it stop.

She stood up and looked at him. He passed her a tissue from his pocket at the sight of the dark streaks under her eyes.

"You think so?" she whispered.

"Absolutely."

"Mm-kay." And with that she made her way back inside.

Logan leaned against the nearest vehicle exhausted from her outburst. After a minute, he phone buzzed in his pocket. He pulled it out and swiped the screen to read the latest text message.

Sophie: *You better not have left. I can't operate those chair stacker thingies.*

He chuckled before texting back. *Just getting some air.*

He shoved his phone back in its place and let out a long sigh. How did he keep ending up with the crazy ones? Couldn't a guy just have some nice company to pass the time without planning for a house with a picket fence? When no immediate answers came to mind, Logan stepped away from the car and made his way back inside much less enthused about the evening. The only thing that could brighten his mood now was a dance with a pretty girl in a sundress.

It took only seconds to spot her wavy blonde tresses floating around the room. But before Logan could approach her at the buffet table, a hand with extraordinarily long, purple fingernails clutched onto his wrist. He turned to the stranger.

A woman nearing forty—or at least a decade his senior—smile up at him maintaining her hold on his arm. "Dance, sugar?" she said.

Logan became dizzy from the sequin top she wore that was the exact colour of her nails, and after a few awkward seconds he remembered he needed to answer her. But she never gave him the chance. She spun quickly and led him to the dance floor. Once there, she sunk her other hand into his shoulder giving him no chance but to assume the dancing position. He reluctantly placed his other hand on her waist. And then Logan decided he had had better nights.

"Can I get your name at least?" he asked uncomfortably.

"Tammy," she said leaning in a little too close.

Logan looked over her shoulder scouring the crowd for anyone that could help him out of this. Drake and Anna were cuddled up close on the dance floor, and Sophie was nowhere to be seen. Just great.

He kept his eyes from meeting Tammy's and tried to focus on the music. The grip she had on his shoulder and his hand were so tight he could barely think straight, let alone recognize the song. He didn't have any problem moving to the beat—music had always come easy for him, but he would've rather done it with a different partner.

SOPHIE watched Logan dance around the hall from the exit doors. She had to giggle at the spectacle. Tammy was chatting up a storm, while Logan's stare followed Drake around the dance floor. He was obviously waiting to flag Drake down for a little assistance with an escape from his current predicament. Sophie could understand the reason Logan was so uncomfortable.

Tammy had been a client with her since almost the start up of her business. She was thirty-nine, had been married twice, and had convinced herself that Mr. Right was definitely not husband number one or number two. She believed that those marriages had been a result of her impatience for settling on a man, nothing more. Sophie was sympathetic toward the woman—she really was looking for love, but the real problem was that her software had produced few men as a match for Tammy. By few, only two men were matches.

And those men had been her ex-husbands.

Regardless of her slim options, Tammy attended every single mixer since Sophie started Match 'Em Up in hopes of snagging another Mr. Right. Sophie had spent plenty of time observing this particular client of hers to see if maybe she could pass on some helpful pointers for the woman. After the third mixer, Sophie politely suggested that she let a man approach her instead. Tammy had argued that she wanted the pick of the litter, not 'the leftovers', which meant she preyed on them the first chance she got. After the sixth mixer, Sophie suggested Tammy minimize the amount of gardenia perfume she wore, since often she left men gasping in her wake...from the smell. Of course, Tammy argued that no man wanted a woman who smelled like laundry detergent because they could smell that at home any time they liked. After that encounter, Sophie stopped with the helpful hints.

Back on the dance floor, Logan had managed to snag Drake's attention, but Sophie watched as Drake smiled huge and waved him off with no intention of helping Logan. She guessed it was time for her to step in and help out a friend.

As she made her way towards the awkward couple, Sophie decided that she would recruit Logan to get a jump-start on the clean up. It was always easier to start during the event, since it left less to do once it was over.

Nearing them, she called out, "Logan—"

Then he did something she didn't expect. He said to Tammy, "Thanks for the, er, lovely dance, Tammy, but I can't pass up a dance with a friend." With a smile, he pried the purple fingernails from his arm and turned to Sophie. His right hand landed on her waist while the other latched on to her hand, and he began twirling her to the music.

Once Sophie was able to regain her bearing from being caught off guard, she placed her hand on his shoulder and followed his lead. She had cleaning in mind, but she supposed a quick dance with a handsome man wouldn't put her behind too much. Plus, his feel for the music was unbelievable, and his moves were even better. Her feet just followed his lead.

"I can't thank you enough," Logan said to her over the music.

Sophie smirked. "For what?"

"From saving me from break up number two of the night."

She shouldn't be surprised with the rumors she heard about his reputation, but the comment still took her aback.

"You were on a roll. I'm sorry I stopped you," she remarked.

Logan stilled in the middle of the dance floor. "You're kidding right?"

"Umm, I guess," she shrugged.

He started them dancing again. "The first one was a surprise. I took her for pizza last night. And she didn't even eat pizza—she had a salad. That hardly counts as a relationship, but according to her, the save the dates should have been ordered by now."

Sophie had no other reply but to laugh. He smiled down at her, clearly enjoying her amusement. The song ended and another one began—this one slower than the last.

Logan began humming along. "I love this song," he whispered between the verse and chorus, spinning her around with ease.

It was one of Sophie's favourites, too. Every time Brett Eldredge's *Mean to Me* came on her radio, she would turn up the volume and sing along. They danced without conversation for a few minutes while Sophie pondered Logan's relationship status and her conversation with Anna the other day about registering Logan as a client again. She couldn't pass up this chance, plus, it would be a good way to keep tabs on her handsome friend.

"You know," she started, "I could help you out of these awkward breakup situations."

He grinned. "Could you now? And how would that be, oh, wise one?"

"By filling out another application—with real answers this time—and becoming a client of Match 'Em Up."

He didn't refuse her outright, but he lost some of the light in his eyes. "I'll think about it," he finally said.

They danced silently until the song came to an end. Logan didn't hum the rest of it with his earlier joviality, and Sophie couldn't help but think that it may have been her fault. She held onto him until he let her go. Regardless of the awkward conversation, being led around the dance floor by Logan was the highlight of her night.

Five

Early Monday morning, Logan lay sprawled under his tractor trying to spot the oil leak with no luck. People thought ranching was picturesque and only a lot of work during calving season, but they were wrong. Logan spent just as much time throughout the year fixing equipment, like tractors and balers, than he did with his cattle. Or so it felt like on mornings like these. He reached for a wrench to start some serious digging. With no tractor, life on his ranch would get very difficult very quickly.

While tinkering with the engine, Logan's mind drifted back to Saturday night. Aside from Carmen's outburst and the more than awkward dance with Tammy, the evening had been one to remember. Five minutes of it had been fantastic. His dance with Sophie had been the best part. Since then, he found his thoughts kept cycling back to her many times a day—morning chores, doing the dishes, catching up on sports highlights late at night.

This had never happened to him with any other woman before, but rather than feel angry or concerned, Logan was enjoying these new feelings. Maybe it was because he was already fond of her as a friend for some time now. He enjoyed her company long before these feelings stirred up, not to mention she was one out of a very small list of woman who had rejected him. Granted, that was in high school. But it could be possible that her being more present in his life lately had dug up his past challenges. Regardless of the reason, Logan was disappointed he didn't ask her out the other night.

After she brought up the subject of him filling out another matchmaking application, he became confused. Did that mean she didn't reciprocate any of his new feelings? Or did she ask him as a friend who cared about his love life? Now, he wished he had come up with a clever way to respond that had resulted in a date with Sophie.

The shop door opened, the sunlight momentarily blinding Logan. Boots and jeans approached the tractor before Mike said, "Need some help down there?"

"Come on down, and bring a flashlight," Logan said with his mind once again on the task at hand.

The two men worked in silence for a while tinkering with this connection, checking that connection. After twenty minutes with no luck finding the leak, they rolled out from under the tractor and began cleaning up the tools. Logan had to head to town later for more parts, so he'd ask the local mechanic if he had any ideas on locating the leak.

"Picked up the mail," Logan said breaking the silence, "Thought I might have seen a birthday card in there."

"You might have seen right," Mike responded.

Logan felt a second of guilt for not remembering his ranch hand's birthday—he could've treated him to lunch or something, but then he remembered that Mike probably spent the weekend celebrating with his own family anyway.

"Have fun with your family then?"

Mike shoved the toolbox drawer closed, and they both moved to the door. "Sure did. Even had cupcakes."

Logan's stomach grumbled reminding him it had been several hours since breakfast. "Bring any back?" he asked.

"Nope. Ate 'em all."

Logan faked a dramatic pout and slugged Mike in the arm. "Think of others who might be suffering next time, man," he joked as they walked to the side-by-side for the morning's herd check.

Every morning one or both men drove the fence line to ensure everything was in place and no calves were caught up in the barbed wire. Logan drove around the property until coming up to the herd, then drove slower as to not spook or disturb any. They found no rebellious calves trying to make an escape today.

On their way back, Mike asked, "What did you do all weekend? I remember you mentioning a date with Carmen, was it?"

Logan sighed. "Yeah, that was a disaster." He relayed the events of Friday night: the menu, the terrible small talk, the awkward drop off, and the inevitable melt down the following night.

Mike howled with laughter at Logan's expense. But he had to admit—it was kind of a funny story.

"How'd you get out of it?"

Logan shrugged. "Told her she deserved someone better."

Mike grunted. "Isn't that the truth?"

"I'm not that bad." Logan jabbed a fist towards Mike's shoulder while thinking of Sophie and wondering if that was actually true. Was he really that bad?

SOPHIE stamped another application as 'Registered' and filed it alphabetically by last name in her current files. With eighteen new applications from Saturday night's mixer, her Monday was looking busy. With twelve new female clients and six men, she was bound to find some successful matches very soon. Reaching for her now cold coffee, she began studying the next application.

Amy Rhodes: twenty-four, moved to this area two years ago to be closer to family, never married, one six-year-old son.

Sophie was sad to see that Amy was a single mother, a job she considered the toughest in the world, but was sure that she had men that would be a match. This was her favourite part of the job—helping people who wanted lasting love to find their soul mates. Although some days she wished that she could find someone for herself.

It would be unethical for her to run her profile with the software and then proceed to date a client. Sophie understood that finding someone for herself would have to be done the old-fashioned way. But a girl could dream. She sometimes found herself reading a man's profile a little too closely and wondering if the man she was setting up with another woman was the person she should pursue. It was too early into her entrepreneurial venture to start being tricky, so on every one of these occasions, Sophie would harness her self-control and continue on as business as usual.

After checking all the desired boxes for Amy's profile, Sophie stamped and filed another application. Just as she was closing her cabinet drawer, a familiar song started playing on the radio catching her attention. It was the same song her and Logan danced to at the mixer the other night.

She hadn't admitted it to anyone, but that dance had been the best part of the night for her. And after the night was over, it left her with a few confusing feelings about her friend.

A black truck pulled up and parked at her storefront. It looked suspiciously like the man in her thoughts, and she confirmed it when his ball cap and broad shoulders came around the back of the vehicle. Sophie watched as he dropped the tailgate and began unloading table after table onto the sidewalk. She had forgotten that he had put them all onto his truck after the mixer on Saturday. He made quick work of the eight tables before closing up the tailgate and heading inside.

Logan greeted her with a charming grin and a polite nod as he wiped his boots off at the door.

"Need some help?" she asked.

"If you could hold the door open, that'd be great."

He grabbed two fold up tables at a time by their handle and stored them in her back room in no time. Sophie was going to have to start paying him for his efforts. Or tip him. Maybe with one of her grandmother's pies—they were basically a local form of currency.

"What 'cha got there?"

Sophie yelped and turned around in her office chair to find Logan reading over her shoulder. Since she had been too busy daydreaming about dancing and pies, Sophie looked back to her computer to check what she had been working on when Logan showed up.

Logan began reading it from behind her. "Jonathan Laymongelo, thirty-two, a convenient store owner, likes everything avian." Logan paused. "What's avian?"

"Birds."

"You're kidding." He reached over her to grab the computer mouse and then scrolled down the page to read the rest of the application. "Pet cockatoo named Stu," he chuckled and turned to look at Sophie with a huge grin, "Stu the Cockatoo."

With that, the two of them doubled over. Soon, Sophie was wiping tears from her cheeks. Once they had their composure back, Logan asked, "Where are you finding these people?"

"Blaine Lake, apparently."

"Read me another."

Sophie huffed. "Logan, I can't. This information isn't just for the general public's viewing pleasure."

He quickly snatched a page off the stack of applicants from Saturday's mixer before she could react. He crossed the room, so she couldn't chase him down and began reading. "Sandra, thirty-seven, hairstylist, likes to bake, loves long walks on the beach—do we even have beaches in Saskatchewan?"

Sophie gave up on trying to retrieve the paper and instead, gathered up the rest of the stack to keep away from him. "Umm, maybe along a lake somewhere."

"I wonder if Stu would like going for long walks on the beach."

"It's Jonathan, actually," Sophie corrected.

Logan smiled. "Right, whatever. It could be a match made in heaven." Sophie faked exasperation. "Well, if you think this is just all a hoax, then maybe you should try following through with that application. I deleted your information from last year, since you only answered three of the questions. Perhaps you would find out that you greatly enjoy long walks on Saskatchewan's non-existent beaches."

Logan looked at her seriously. "As a matter of fact, that is the very opposite reason I find myself in your office right now."

Sophie stiffened. "What's the real reason?"

What seemed like minutes of silence passed as she waited for him to elaborate, when in fact, it was mere seconds. "I should've asked you out on Saturday, so I wanted to now."

Sophie sat stunned. He hadn't asked her out since high school, and she assumed he would never do it again after she gave him refusal after refusal. But something about the way he said it just now told her that this time was different. She detected a lot of sincerity in his statement, something she had never heard before when he turned his charm on for a woman. Logan always made it clear that the date would be casual, nothing serious. But this time, the statement had a bit of weight to it. And she had no idea what to say. With the dance from the other night still fresh in her mind, Sophie's immediately reaction would be to say yes. But his reputation preceded him, and she wasn't looking to ruin the friendship they had built lately.

Finally, she said, "I'm not quite sure what to say."

Sophie watched as Logan fidgeted with his hands then adjusted his hat. She hadn't ever seen him nervous before.

"You could say yes."

"Umm—" Sophie created a mental pros and cons list while he waited for an answer, but apparently, she was taking too long.

"I'll tell you what," he started, "I'll fill out one of those silly things again—for real this time," he said gesturing with air quotes, "and become a client if you agree to a date."

"I don't date clients," she replied immediately.

Logan was quick with a rebuttal. "But you're forcing me, so it doesn't count."

"If you become a client, you'll have matches. And dates," she argued.

"Fine, the town seems to think that my first dates never lead to a second anyway."

Something about his response alerted Sophie that Logan was none too pleased about what Sethburn thought of him. Maybe 'Match 'Em Up' could help him with that.

"One date?" she confirmed.

"With you."

"'Kay."

Six

Logan kicked off his boots in the mudroom while he stripped off his jacket and gloves. It had been pouring rain all morning, and he was sure that the boots weighed a few more pounds then when he had first put them on an hour ago. He shivered as the air hit his wet shirt and socks. It was time for a second cup of extra hot coffee and some breakfast.

While the coffee brewed, he toasted a whole-wheat bagel and smothered it with cream cheese. He took both to the table and sat down. As he inhaled the bagel and downed the coffee between bites, Logan eyed the blank application he was supposed to fill out for Sophie at the far end of the table. Last night he had stared at it for fifteen minutes without writing a single thing down—not even his name. It was harder this time since his answers needed to be thought out. All he could think about was why he had agreed to Sophie's deal in the first place. For some reason, with her he wanted it to be different, and he wasn't sure why. Maybe he wanted to prove his reputation was fictional…or at least that he could change and prove the people of Sethburn wrong.

He wanted a chance with this girl. It went against everything he believed for the last decade. It scared him to no end that this would end up as the same situation from his childhood, but Logan just couldn't walk away from Sophie without a real date, a real chance. He was confused and stressed, and he needed to talk to his father. Lincoln always seemed to have sound advice at the ready for his son. Logan mentally put that on his to-do list and reached for a pen.

Full Name: Logan James Fraser

Birthdate: April 6, 1988

Age Preference for Matches: 23-30

Level of Education: Diploma of Agricultural Studies

Occupation: Cattle Rancher

And so it went for the first page. Logan easily answered the simple questions and wondered if it had really been this easy last time. Was this all it took to find a soul mate? It sure didn't seem like qualifying criteria to produce a person that someone could spend the rest of their life with, but he forged on and turned the page.

How do you spend weekday evenings? Watching football or hockey at home. With friends at home or restaurant.

What type of books do you read? Thrillers, mysteries

What is your greatest achievement? Making my father proud when taking over his ranch.

These questions were lengthier but just as easy to answer as the ones before. Logan checked his watch and determined he might as well finish this up before meeting Mike in the shop to inspect the baler and replace the belts. Surely an hour would be plenty enough time to finish it. Last time, he hadn't spent more than ten minutes scribbling responses down.

Where do you see yourself in five years?

Logan sat back to think about the question. Truly, he pictured himself in the exact same house with the exact same career. What he couldn't picture was if he would be sharing that with anyone. He read the next question without answering the last. He would come back to it.

What is the most important part of a marriage?

Again, Logan stared at the question without an answer. Instead, he wondered what would have helped his parents, what would have been the key to his mother never wanting to leave? He jotted down what came to mind and moved to the next question without dwelling too deeply on his past. This was turning into a more difficult process then he first anticipated. He didn't remember any of these questions from the first time.

What are your spiritual beliefs and how do you practice them?

Logan thought back to his past—one of his most vivid memories. The three of them had been sitting at the dinner table after they had finished the meal. His father was reading from a children's devotional book. The lesson had been on love. Logan remember his dad saying, "Just as your parents love you even when you make a mistake, Jesus loves you the same way. He loves you even more than you can imagine."

That night Logan had prayed with his parents and accepted Jesus into his heart. He was seven. For the next nine years, Logan attended Sunday school and youth group growing in his faith, trusting God for life's answers, and leaning on Him in times of need. But just weeks after his sixteenth birthday, everything changed, including Logan's beliefs.

How could God let his mother leave like that? How could God ruin him and his father's lives? Lincoln and Logan had moved to Sethburn only months after his mother left. He left his friends, his home, his church, and his God behind. Now, Lincoln insisted that

Logan go to church only a few times a year—Easter, Christmas, and a few Sundays in between when his father was in the mood to drag him there. Logan was glad that his father didn't push him to regularly attend, but it was obvious that Lincoln still lived his faith and never hid it from anyone, especially Logan.

Logan stared at the question once more. Sophie would be reading this, and she would probably be able to tell if he was being truthful or not, so not answering these questions was not an option. He promised her more this time around. He wrote a few words then hastily scratched them out. He tried again and wrote a few sentences. Satisfied, Logan continued onto the next question.

Thirty minutes later as Logan scribbled in his last answer on the application, his cell phone rang. He checked the caller ID and answered, "Hey, Mike."

"Logan," he greeted, "Eighty-four's all twisted up in the fence again."

Logan was already on his way to the mudroom. "Where at?"

"South corner, 'bout three hundred feet from where she was caught up last time."

Logan grabbed the keys to his side-by-side. "Be there in ten."

He put the thoughts of that application and Sophie to the back of his mind on the way out to the pasture. He let the wind blow all the stress of reliving some of his past away and set his eyes on the fence line in search of Mike.

Eighty-four hadn't been so lucky this time. They freed her from the barbed wire only to find a large gash on one of her hind legs. It wasn't something that would heal on its own, so Logan and Mike carted her to the yard on the back of the side by side. It took a few tries to get the ornery calf into the stock trailer, but with Lincoln's help they managed to have her loaded by noon. Logan made a quick change of clothes—he didn't think walking around with blood on his jeans would bode well while in town—and swiped his Match 'Em Up application off the table on the way out the door. Two birds with one stone and all that.

It took a shorter time to unload the calf at the vet because Anita, the veterinarian technician, seemed to be an animal whisperer. It was good news for Logan because the bagel he had hours earlier had long been used up. After finding a parking space long enough for his truck and trailer, he ordered a coffee and a cinnamon bun from Flatlands.

As he walked the single block to Sophie's office with his application in hand, Logan recalled his answers to some of the more difficult questions, and he wondered what Sophie would think of his very truthful explanations. He worried that maybe the whole deal would be off after she read what he had written. It was a known Sethburn fact that the Rempels were recognizable by their unwavering faith—a quality he did not share with the woman in his thoughts. So instead of stepping inside to say hello and risk interrogation, Logan slid the paper through the mail slot and returned to his truck. He had a fence to fix, anyway.

SOPHIE came from tidying the back room to the front office when she heard the mail drop. It seemed too early for her regular mail man—she would know with having worked at the post office for six years, but she was waiting on a parcel and wanted to check for it right away. Without even reaching the door, Sophie could tell it wasn't the matchmaking books she ordered, but not wanting to go back to cleaning, she reached down for the papers.

She turned it over and immediately noted Logan's name on the top of the application. Her curiosity was peaked. She sat and rolled her office chair up to her computer. It was time to enter her latest client into the database.

The first page of general questions established the majority of the matches, and once the software included the more in depth information, more specific matches were generated, eliminating many of the superficial similarities. After reading through Logan's answers, it was obvious he would have lots to choose from. And she noticed that he definitely took more time than last year to fill it out. The next page held some surprising answers. Sophie hadn't known that Logan's five-year plan consisted solely of expanding the ranch. He didn't hint at the subject of family at all, which was unusual for other clients in that age range. She shouldn't have been surprised given his reputation with Sethburn's female population, but almost all clients planned to settle down by thirty.

Sophie entered his answers and checked the appropriate boxes, than moved down the list. His answers regarding friendships were charming. His response to building lasting friendships was to invite them to share a meal while a sports game played on mute and good music filled in the background. That actually sounded like a pretty perfect date to her.

With no mention of family on his previous answers, Sophie was surprised to read what he wrote about the qualities of a good marriage. His answer was commitment. It was the only word written down, and it struck her. How could a man whose name was known for casual relationships that never went past a few dates believe that commitment was the most important quality of a marriage? It was puzzling, but amidst the confusion of his answer, Sophie felt assured that Logan's capacity for relationships was much larger than he let on. It also meant that his past might have many layers that had yet to be discovered.

But just as Sophie reshaped the view of her friend to a more positive one, Logan's final answer about his spiritual beliefs stunted what had begun to grow.

Growing up in a Christian home where parents read devotions at the dinner table, take you to church on Sundays, and take you to and from youth group every Tuesday night does not mean that your future includes God. It didn't for me. I respect people's need for faith, I don't admonish what they do, but I don't believe in His so called 'plans', in His unconditional love, and His brand of justice. I have personal experience of having hope in Him then having dreams become nothing but ashes. I don't believe in any god. I don't practice a faith. And I don't begrudge those who do.

Sophie sat dazed staring at Logan's explanation. She didn't know much about his past. She had a basic understanding that only Logan and his father moved to Sethburn and that his mother was never mentioned. It was obvious Logan had been hurt deeply enough to give up his faith, and the sadness in his statement made Sophie's heart ache for him. Whatever he had gone through had been devastating, it had ruined close relationships, it had ruined his family. Right then, Sophie realized her friendship with this man had always been superficial. Surface. And after reading his application, she wanted to know Logan, truly. She wanted to dig into the reasons he had abandoned Jesus, and just maybe, God would grant her an opportunity to reveal to Logan that the faith his left behind was the faith he needed to heal.

Once she was finished entering Logan's information into her software, Sophie questioned whether it had been wrong for her to agree to a date with him only if he submitted an application. She had used it as a bargaining chip to expand her client base and take on the fun project of finding love for the one man who wanted the opposite. She had quite a dilemma, and she knew only one person who could help her out of that.

Exactly thirty minutes later Sophie sat down across from her grandmother in one of Flatlands' cushy, outdated booths. Grandma Faye had had a huge part in Anna's move back to Sethburn and her rekindled relationship with Drake last year. Her eighty-three years of wisdom could solve almost any problem, and Sophie was about to ask for some advice of her own.

Sheila made quick work of pouring a cup of coffee for Sophie and bringing Faye a steaming cup of Earl Grey tea.

"Morning, Grandma."

"Dear," she exchanged, "it's been two weeks since I've seen you around, which means business must be good."

Sophie was glad her grandmother never held time against her; instead, she understood from the moment Sophie came up with her business idea and had even offered to help with whatever the business needed. She accepted Sophie's busy days, and when they were together, Faye never complained about their time apart. It made it a much happier time when they managed to spend time together like today. And because of their great times together, Sophie always aimed to see her grandmother at least a few times a month.

"So busy. We wrapped up the monthly mixer Saturday night. It was a huge success—the biggest turn out yet. I'm so glad I have Anna to help with the catering and decorating."

"That's great, dear. I never doubted a single mixer's success. Sethburn needs more families, more love, and you're just the girl to make that happen." She winked before sipping her tea.

Sophie poured two creams in her mug. "But I actually wanted to talk about something else with you today."

Faye hummed. "Sounds interesting."

Sophie launched into her dilemma. She explained her recent interest in Logan, their dance and fun banter at the mixer, their little wager with it ending in her agreeing to a date. She finished with Logan's gloomy answer regarding his stance on God and faith.

"What should I do, Gran?"

"It's certainly a lot to take in all at once. Let's start at the beginning."

Sophie nodded awaiting Faye's sound prudence. .

"First of all, Logan is a fine young man. Hard worker, respects his father. Handsome, too," she added with a chuckle.

"He is that," Sophie agreed.

"I think it's good that you are concerned about him. It's good that you want to help him heal from whatever is broken."

Sophie felt a 'but' coming, and Faye didn't disappoint.

"But, I think that wager was a little ridiculous."

Sophie moaned. "I knew that was a bad idea."

Faye reached across the table for Sophie's hand. Once it covered hers comfort enveloped her like a blanket.

"Not really. Just silly. But, dear, you have an opportunity right now to be his friend even if he is a client of yours. A friend who wants to help him. Take that for what it is this very minute, and if God has a plan for you two, it will come with time."

Sophie smiled. "You promise?"

"No," Faye laughed, "but the Bible does."

"That is exactly what I needed to hear."

"Good."

And with that, they moved onto the subject of the pesky dandelions Faye was trying to eradicate from her lawn.

SOPHIE pulled up seventeen possible matches for one Logan Fraser—the highest she had even seen since starting Match 'Em Up had been nine. Logan had *seventeen*. Last year, his results were nowhere near that many since she didn't have as many clients, and since he hadn't spent the time on the application, she doubted he would have had more than a few anyway.

She scrolled through the entire list, noting several women he had already been on a date with—that she knew of, so she shrunk the list to twelve. Sophie checked off the most compatible of the twelve. Isla was a nurse from two counties over, whose favourite colour was 'rainbow', go figure. Hannah was a lunch monitor at

Sethburn's elementary school, who drove a John Deere gator to and from work, winter or summer. Peyton ran the local animal shelter, and had a Rottweiler named Oscar she took everywhere with her. Olivia was the area's only ballet teacher, and Sophie knew by the picture she submitted that Olivia was the same woman she saw tiptoeing down the cereal aisle last week. Amy was a receptionist and single mother who was new to the area and looking to meet new people. And Maeve was a librarian slash Roughriders fan that clearly stated in her application she wouldn't date anyone who was cheering against the green.

As Sophie waded through the information to find the closest match, her grandmother's advice weighed on her mind. Yes, she had agreed to a date with Logan, and she would go. It would be a time for Sophie to get to know him on a deeper level than pancake eating contests and two-stepping. The possibility of one-on-one time might provide the right circumstances for an open conversation. She hoped it led to more time with him—time long enough to ease pains of the past and restore his hope for the future.

But first, she had to find him a match.

Seven

Logan's arms would be sore when the day was done. Even with Mike's help for the last three hours, they were still no closer to replacing the belts on his baler. Two of the belts had gotten cut, then jammed inside the motor on the trial run Logan had taken yesterday. With only a few hours left before Mike would leave for the weekend, Logan wondered if this project would ever get done. He was running out of bales he stocked from last fall, so it was crucial that he get this machine in working order. His hay crop was already knee-deep, which meant it was time to bale the first round this season.

Both men stepped back to wipe their brows. June temperatures had snuck up on them putting the shop well over twenty-five degrees.

"You mean to tell me the charming Logan Fraser does not have a date tonight?" Mike teased.

In the last hour their conversation had veered away from the baler problems while they worked, and the subject had landed on Logan's dating life.

"Nothing on the agenda." Logan lifted his ball cap to wipe the rest of the sweat from his forehead.

"I can see why, though. Who would want to date a sweaty mess?"

Logan laughed. "That doesn't say much for you either."

Both men stared down at their clothes. Greasy smudges covered their jeans and shirts. Sweat caused dark shadows under their arms and down their backs. They looked at each other and laughed.

Once they were able to control themselves again, they got back to work.

"But seriously, man, no date? That's not like you."

Logan sighed. It was time he told Mike what was going on with Sophie. "Well, there's this one girl—," he started.

"One? That's not the Logan I know," Mike butted in.

Logan punched him in the arm. "Would you let me finish?"

Mike chuckled. "Yeah, yeah. Go on."

"You remember Sophie, right? The matchmaker."

"Sure, yeah. The pancake eater."

Logan laughed. He guessed Sophie wouldn't be too pleased to learn that she was known for her eating competition skills. "That's her. Anyway, she rejected me in high school a bunch of times. She and Anna, her sister, were the two girls I could never get to go out with me—not one time. Well, now that Anna and Drake are getting married, we all tend to spend a lot of time together. And last weekend, I helped her out with her mixer event. She saved me from this older woman who was stake her claim on me. We ended up dancing—"

"You dance?" Mike cut in again.

"I dance," Logan said defensively.

"Okay, okay. Carry on."

Logan huffed at the interruption but continued. "We danced and talked. She's great, not at all what I originally thought she'd be like. The pancakes and the dancing proved that. We ended up making this deal. I have to become a client at Match 'Em Up, and she agreed to a date."

"That is the weirdest thing I have ever heard of."

"Yeah, well, me too. I think I blew it though. She made me fill out one of those really long questionnaires. I did one last year, but refused to follow through with the dates when she called a few weeks later. There were some tough questions on there, and I'm fairly certain that she'll hate what I had to say."

"Then why'd you say it?"

"She said answer truthfully and thoroughly this time, and if I ever wanted a second date with this girl I wanted to start off on the right foot. Besides, why would I want to go out with her if she doesn't approve of my answers? Then there's really no point. I wouldn't have to suffer through blind dates, and she wouldn't have to date me. The deal would be off."

"When do you find out if you've got yourself a date?"

Just then Mike's cell phone rang, and he hopped off the top of the machine to answer it. The reception in the shop wasn't good, so he headed to the door.

Logan overheard a bit of the conversation.

"Is he alright? Yes. Yeah, I'll pick some up. Okay, I'll be over if a couple of hours. 'Bye."

Just as Mike made his way back to the workstation, Logan's phone rang. The two smirked at each other over the situation as Logan headed for the door this time.

"Hello."

"Hey there. It's Sophie."

Logan smiled. It was time to cash in that date. "Ready to make good on the rest of our deal?"

"Actually, no."

Logan stopped at the door, puzzled. "You can't back out now. I already did my part."

"Not all of it," she said.

He didn't like the sound of that. "Meaning?"

"It means you'll be meeting Maeve Montgomery at the Wagon Wheel tonight at seven for your first date."

Logan pinched the bridge of his nose. "You're kidding."

"Nope," she said way too cheerfully. "It took me two days to get this set up. You're going. And you'll be nice to Maeve."

Logan admitted defeat. He wanted a date with Sophie, so he'd endure an evening with this Maeve character if he had to. "How will I know what she looks like?"

"I'll text you her profile picture."

"Fantastic," he added sarcastically.

"I will call you first thing tomorrow to see how it went."

"Don't forget you owe me."

He heard her sigh on the other end of the phone. "I know. 'Bye."

As soon as he ended the call, his phone dinged alerting him of a text message. He opened the picture and studied the picture.

"I guess you've got plans after all," Mike called from inside the baler.

But with the wrong woman.

ON the short drive to the Wagon Wheel, Logan did not think about the woman he was about to spend the evening with. Instead, the woman on his mind was the woman who had set up the date. Her earlier reluctance to schedule their time together was bothering Logan, and he could all but guess it might have something to do with his application.

He had been rather blunt about what he thought of the faith that Sophie had. Not rude, but his answer had definitely been straightforward—he didn't believe. He didn't regret the way he answered that question, and he hoped when he was finally about to spend some one-on-one time with Sophie that he could convince her that a true god wouldn't separate a family like what had happened to his own. He was sure Sophie would understand his reasoning.

He pulled up to the restaurant about ten minutes early, so he went inside to get him and his date a table. He sat down facing the door so he could wave Maeve over once she arrived. Logan took a second look at the picture of Maeve Sophie had texted him—petite, long, dark hair, simple. He admitted that it wasn't someone he would typically ask out, but he supposed that was the entire point of this endeavor that was Match 'Em Up.

The door chimed, and Logan recognized her immediately. Not because of the picture Sophie had sent but because he remembered her wearing the very same shirt at the mixer only six days before. It was an unassuming green t-shirt with a large Saskatchewan Roughriders logo on it. At least he knew they had one common interest. He waved her over to the table.

She didn't wait for Logan to stand and introduce himself. No, instead she plopped down with little grace while hooking her purse strap to the chair knob behind her. Then she stuck out her hand across the table for a handshake. Not sure what to think of the abrupt first impression, Logan did the only thing he could think of. He clasped her hand and hoped for the best.

Her shake was firm and to the point. "You're Logan."

It wasn't a question. She just simply told him his name, so he returned the favour. "You're Maeve."

The waitress interrupted them before anything else was said. "To drink?"

Maeve asked for a Coke, and Logan asked for the same. The day spent in a baler had worked up a lot of thirst, and a cold cola was the thing to quench it. Instead of picking up a conversation, Maeve dove into the menu, reading every item thoroughly. Logan didn't want to disrupt her choosing process, so he perused his own. The Wagon Wheel was the restaurant Sethburnians went to when they weren't in the mood for Flatlands' breakfast menu. This place served almost everything, but their specialty was good ol' Mennonite cooking.

Logan hadn't been introduced to this type of cholesterol raising, artery plugging goodness until he made the move to Sethburn, but he was sure glad Drake had brought him here one Thursday after school. He had eaten eight cottage cheese perogies, two links of farmer sausage, and half an order of Kielke—home-style noodles smothered in cream gravy. It was still the best meal he had ever eaten. Today, he decided on just one serving of perogies and farmer sausage since his digestive system was just about a decade older than the first time he had eaten here. Maeve chose the bison burger with a side of fries. Logan had seen the size of that burger come out of the kitchen before, and he wondered if it could possibly outweigh his date. Maybe this evening would be more entertaining that he thought.

"So you like football, I see." It had been a lame attempt at starting a conversation, but it was the best Logan could come up with.

She nodded excitedly while sipping her pop. "Sure do, first regular season game is tomorrow. I hope Durant's injury recovery is game worthy. Without our star quarterback, I start to worry about our offense. I mean, our defense is solid with Chick always on the leaderboard for quarterback sacks, but we need to score too, you know? With White retiring and a few ill-advised trades in the off season, I'm excited to see what the coach does with the new roster."

Logan was a bit awestruck with Maeve's knowledge of his favourite sport. Not many women he met could speak intelligently about Canadian football. It was great that they shared a favourite team.

Logan added his own opinion. "I don't think you should count out our offense just yet. Durant's had plenty of recovery time, the backup is decent, and with running backs like Allen and Ford, we've got something to build on with our rushing game. If the quarterback can't put up long throws, he can at least pass it off to guys that have some legs to them."

Their football talk continued until the food arrived. Logan had already determined he and Maeve would never have a love connection, but they would be game day buddies in the future—he was sure of that. He also owed Sophie an apology for being leery about tonight. Even though there wouldn't be a second date, he was enjoying Maeve's company.

Once their plates had been cleared and the dessert order had been placed, Logan asked a question that had been weighing on his mind since filling out an application to a matchmaking service.

"So Maeve, why did you sign up for Match 'Em Up?"

She was quiet for a moment developing her answer. "My brother signed me up actually. I'm a librarian, so if my nose isn't in a book, I'm usually watching sports. I don't have very many friends, I keep to myself a lot. He thought it might be good for me."

Logan digested her response. He appreciated her brother's good intentions and gained a new level of understanding for Sophie's business. Maeve was great company and would be someone's match one day, he was certain. So in this case, Match

'Em Up was a great way to help out. It was obvious that he had misjudged the matchmaking business. Even though it still wasn't for him, he now understood it was an effective way for others to meet their match.

Logan and Maeve exchanged numbers as they left the restaurant and made plans to watch a Riders game together within the next few weeks. Logan started the evening skeptical and not in the mood to forge a connection, but he drove home happy he made a new friend.

Once he was placed in front of the television with the day's sport highlights turned on, Logan reached for his phone. He wanted to tell Sophie about his night.

She picked up on the third ring. "Logan?"

"Hey. Are you busy?" He heard voices in the background and didn't want to interrupt her Friday night.

"Not at all. Just watching a movie. I'll pause it." The noise disappeared.

"New or a re-watch?"

"Re-watch. Parent Trap—the original. It's been my favourite since the first time I watched it when I was a girl."

Logan laughed. It wasn't really his type of movie. "I never pegged you for an oldies type."

"You've got a lot to learn."

"So I do," he teased.

"Wait a minute. You're supposed to be on a date."

"Before you yell at me, I just got home. It was fun."

"Yeah? You and Maeve hit it off?" she asked clearly surprised.

Logan hesitated as he tried to find the right words. "We both really love football, but that's about the only love connection of the night. We did make plans to watch a game together though."

"Well, that's something I guess."

Logan couldn't help but notice Sophie sounded a little too upbeat about the results of the date, so he went for broke. "Our date will have a better ending. I promise."

Sophie giggled. "You sound sure of yourself."

"I am," he said, "Just tell me the time and place so I can prove it to you."

"Hmm, sounds exciting."

Sophie started listing her weekend schedule. She and Anna had offered to help her parents with yard work the next day. Her mother had booked Sunday as family day, starting with church, then lunch, then an afternoon and evening of games, movies, and fun in the kitchen. After Logan heard the list, they agreed to postpone scheduling any time together. Logan's disappointment had disappeared as soon as he heard the enthusiasm in Sophie's voice about the weekend. He was happy she would be spending it with her family, so he would just have to wait a little longer.

Eight

Sophie ended the call with Logan and stayed sitting on the couch recalling their quick conversation. She was glad to hear that Logan's opinion of her business was changing, and surprised that Maeve and Logan had become friends over the course of the evening since Logan had been skeptical about the matchmaking process. It wasn't always about a love connection; it was also a great way to make new friends. She was glad that he had put some effort into the evening even if it had been for the sake of holding up his end of the bargain.

The call settled her nerves that had been weighing on her all evening. Only for the past few hours had Sophie considered the potential results of Logan going on dates with other women while she was trying to build her own bond with him. She kept wondering what would happen if Logan found a woman worthy of his commitment before he and Sophie had a chance to build their own relationship? The thought hadn't crossed her mind when she first came up with the idea because Logan had never expressed interest in having a real relationship with any woman. His reputation held evidence that he dated women only a few times before moving on to the next one.

But Logan's teasing about their own upcoming date pushed back all the questions that had stirred up her anxiety. His excitement about their future plans was palpable even over the phone. Sophie couldn't wait to finalize a plan and get to know him better. She'd been praying all week that there would be a chance to share about Jesus with Logan, and even though it might not be on their first date, she was willing to wait for the right time.

Anna came from the kitchen with two steaming mugs of hot chocolate. Sophie's was filled to the brim with marshmallows— just the way she liked it.

"Was that Mom on the phone asking about tomorrow's yard work schedule?" Anna asked as she sat down.

"No, it was Logan actually." Anna had been busy with Drake all week finalizing wedding plans and tracking down the late RSVPs, which meant Sophie hadn't told her about what had happened between herself and Logan.

Anna's eyebrows rose at Sophie's response. "Since when does Logan call at," she checked her watch, "nine-thirty in the evening?"

Sophie laughed at her sister's exaggeration. "Since he became my client and went out with his first match tonight."

"You mean he actually filled out an application this time? As in answered all the questions instead of just the first page? Surely, you mean someone else," Anna said only half kidding.

"Well, there's a catch."

"A catch?"

Sophie explained the agreement she had made with Logan. He would become a Match 'Em Up client, and she agreed to go on a date with him.

"I can't believe he went through with it, Anna. I anticipated him thinking the application and blind dates would be too much work just for one measly date with me. But he's gone through all this trouble already, and we haven't even been out yet."

Anna sat across from her thinking over everything Sophie had revealed. "You know what I think?"

Sophie nodded.

"I think Logan has a crush on my sister," Anna said with a grin.

Sophie laughed at the childish statement, but at the same time, she hoped it held a little truth.

"Think so?"

"Why not?"

"I keep reminding myself of high school and the times he asked me out then. It was several, and I said no every time. You don't think he just wants to improve his record?"

Anna threw back her head with a laugh. "Not a chance. That would be a lot of work for a single date. He's into you, Soph."

"There's just one problem," Sophie added.

Anna nodded with understanding. Logan didn't share her faith. "Drake has tried to get him to church, but he refuses. The times he does make an appearance are special holidays, and Drake told me that's only because Lincoln's asks him to come on those days."

Both women sighed. "I've been thinking a lot about this very situation during the last week. I think this date could be a chance for me to build a real friendship with him. We've been talking more lately, and I can say that I have developed a little crush on him too. I want him to know Jesus even if he is just a friend."

"I think that's a great idea."

Sophie sensed there was a 'but'.

"But I want you to be careful. Everyone knows about his reputation. And Drake knows about his reluctance to attend church or explore a relationship with God. I don't want to see you end up with a broken heart."

"I don't either. But Logan needs a chance to feel God's love, and then maybe he'd be more open to other love."

Anna leaned over to hug her sister. "I hope you're right. I'll be praying for both of you."

SOPHIE could barely hear the country music blasting through her headphones above the noise of the lawnmower, but that was just how she liked it. Ever since she was tall enough to reach the pedals, mowing her parents' lawn had been the only chore she truly enjoyed. Her Walkman, her Discman, her MP3 player, and now her iPod had become some of her best summer companions while on the lawn tractor. Today, Luke Bryan sang to her from the speakers, and she sang right along with him. Or tried, anyway.

Their lawn was just shy of two acres, which meant mowing took almost two hours. Sophie had started just after eight this morning to beat the heat and had only a quarter of it left. She turned the tractor around to head back down the lawn when a truck turned into the driveway. Seconds later, she realized it was Logan's pick-up that was now parking in front of her parents' house.

She looked down at herself. Her bare legs were covered in grass and dust. Her jean shorts looked about the same. She touched her hair and felt all the grass that had taken up residence in her ponytail. Sophie could only imagine how dusty her face was. It was not the ideal time to be seeing Logan. But there was nothing she could do about it now. Her parents and Anna had disappeared behind the house to work on her mother's garden, which meant she was the only one there to greet him. She turned around at the edge of the lawn and made her way back towards the house.

After powering down the blades and the tractor, she dusted herself off as best she could.

"Mornin'," Logan drawled as he climbed out of the truck.

"Hey, there. I didn't know you were stopping by today." By now she stood just a few foot from him.

He looked at her closely. "You've got a little something—," he motioned to her nose.

Sophie swiped at it vigorously. Her hands came away full of dirt and grime. "Oh, gross. Come to the house. I've got to wash this off," she said as she marched to the door. How embarrassing.

Logan chuckled behind her. "You're still pretty easy on the eyes under all that dirt," he said as he caught up to her.

They both took off their boots in the entryway, and Logan followed her to the kitchen. The aroma of cinnamon buns filled the air just as she heard Logan's stomach rumble.

"Hungry?" she asked with a smirk.

"Now? Yes." He laughed.

"I'm sure Mom wouldn't mind. Help yourself," she gestured on her way to the sink.

She took a good minute to rinse off her face and wash her hands. Her hair would have to wait.

"Better?" she asked turning to face him.

Logan smiled. "Didn't say it was bad before."

Sophie blushed at the compliment. "Want a drink with that?"

Logan was almost through the whole cinnamon bun already, but she understood the need to eat quickly—her mother's recipe was *that* good. Sophie thought they were better than her Grandma Faye's apple pie, but she had never summoned the courage to speak that aloud. She was afraid it might divide the family.

"Milk, please," he said between bites.

She poured him a glass of milk and a cup of iced tea for herself.
"So you never told me why you actually stopped by."

Logan licked his fingers clean. "Anna texted me yesterday asking for some baler twine—something about wedding favors. I have no idea what that actually means, but I brought her three hundred feet of it."

Sophie laughed at his wedding naivety. She knew immediately what it was for. Anna and Grandma Faye made two hundred small jars of homemade apple jam a week ago to be given out as favors to the wedding guests. The baler twine would be used to tie the cute plaid fabric over the lid of the jars.

"That was nice of you. Weddings are so expensive, and I know Anna is trying to save money wherever she can."

Logan shrugged. "No biggie."

Sophie's phone chirped with an incoming message, and she checked the screen.

"Oh, good thing I had this reminder set. I forgot to call to tell you last night that your second date is Tuesday night. I hope that works for you."

Logan raised his eyebrows at her statement. "That was quick."

Sophie couldn't help but feel nervous at his reaction. He was doing all this just for time with her, and she hadn't found a way out for both of them yet. Match 'Em Up applications clearly stated that a minimum of three dates was required. She had, however, managed to arrange three dates with Logan's matches all within a little over a week. She figured he would appreciate getting it over with.

"Her name is Olivia. She's a ballet teacher originally from Regina. You'll be attending her nephew's middle school baseball game."

Logan was quiet for a minute. "I'd rather be going on a date with you, but okay."

His acceptance and compliment made her smile. "Just two more, Logan. The application says a minimum of three. Then you're done."

"Promise?"

"You make it sound like these dates are torture. I thought you liked dating," she joked.

"Promise?" he repeated.

"Promise."

"Anywhere in the fine print say I can't take you out before my three dates are over with?" he asked.

"It does not, which you would know if you'd read it more thoroughly last time," she teased.

"Good. Thursday, my place. I'll make you dinner."

Sophie didn't even bother to check her schedule. "'Kay."

LOGAN drove to Sethburn's only baseball diamond on Tuesday evening. Since Saturday, he had been counting down the days—no, hours—until Thursday's plans with Sophie. And tonight's outing was just one more obstacle in the way.

When Sophie reminded him on the weekend about the three-date clause on the matchmaking application, he had mixed emotions. He was annoyed that he still had two more unnecessary dates to endure, but he was glad to see the light at the end of the tunnel. He was more certain since Sophie had been eager to schedule their own time together that her feelings would reciprocate his. They both wanted to get to know each other better, and the clause was getting in the way of that.

Logan couldn't wait until Thursday.

As he turned into the parking lot, gravel crunched under the tires while he looked for a spot. He dodged pothole after pothole on the gravel lot until he found a space and pulled in. This diamond was used almost every evening during the summer, yet the town had yet to pave the lot. He'd have to bring that up at the next city council meeting. He reached into his pocket for his phone to make a note of it.

Just as he began to type it out, his shoulder collided with something—no, someone. She fell to the ground, landing on her hands and knees with an 'ooph'.

Logan spun around and lowered himself to her side. "Are you alright? I'm so sorry."

Curly, blonde hair shielded her face from his view, so he reached for her arm to help her up.

"I'm, uh, okay. I think." She tucked her hair behind her ears as she stood.

Seeing her face, Logan determined he had been very wrong about her age. The woman was so small, barely reaching the middle of his chest, which was why his initial guess had been that she was just a girl. He guessed her height to be right around five feet.

"You sure? Your knees okay? Let me see your hands." Logan reached for them. A few minor scratches were etched on her palms, but no blood was drawn.

"I'll get you some ice," he decided. "Follow me."

He ushered them both to the canteen and asked the teen working behind the counter for some ice. While they waited, he introduced himself, "I'm Logan, by the way."

The woman snorted. "Of course you are."

"Excuse me?"

"I'm Olivia."

Logan groaned. "What a first impression I've made. Can I apologize again?" He grabbed the ice from the boy and gently pressed some to each hand.

Olivia laughed. "No need. Your help is enough. I'm usually more graceful than this."

They began making their way to the bleachers behind the backstop as the players took the field.

"That's right. Sophie told me you are a dance teacher."

"Yes. Ballet. So you would've thought I could stick the landing back there."

They laughed together as they found a seat.

Two umpires and a young girl walked to the pitcher's mound as the teams lined up along the first and third baselines. One of the umpires spoke into the microphone. "Please remove your hats for the singing of 'O Canada.'"

Logan took his ball cap off as the canned organ began to play through the speakers. He sang every word from memory, enjoying the tradition of Canadian sports events.

When the anthem ended, they took their seats. Olivia leaned toward him and said, "You have a beautiful voice."

Logan blushed. It had been awhile since anyone had heard him sing. "Thanks," he mumbled.

The innings flew by, and Olivia's nephew hit two singles and a triple by the ninth inning. Their team had last bat and were down by one run as the other team took the field. Logan tried to pay attention the best he could, but he had music on his mind. He had been so busy in the last few weeks, he was sure his guitar had gathered a layer of dust. Maybe if the evening ended early enough, he would have some time before the night was over to play a little. He had noted a few new songs on the radio last week he wanted to attempt.

The home team managed two runs before getting three out and took the win. Olivia rushed down the bleachers with the other parents and fans to congratulate the team, and Logan followed slowly behind.

Their conversation had been friendly during the game, and stayed on surface level topics like weather, jobs, and the baseball game. If he didn't have a different beautiful blonde on his mind, Logan might have requested a second date with Olivia. But the evening had done nothing to deter his excitement for Thursday night.

When the team celebration winded down, Olivia found him in the crowd.

"Great game, huh?" she said.

Logan smiled. It had been fun to watch—what he could remember of it, anyway. "Great game," he agreed.

Olivia hesitated before speaking again. "I heard some things about you before."

Logan's shoulders slumped as he dreaded what he was about to hear. "Like what?"

"I had heard you were overly charming, but never made any promises. Or second dates."

He winced. "That sounds about a right. Did I ruin your night?" He apologized in advance even though, ordinarily, he would have said the evening was a success.

Olivia laughed. "You didn't ruin anything, but I am getting the vibe that date number two is probably off the table."

Logan grimaced again. "Olivia, it has nothing to do with tonight. I promise. I just—" he almost mentioned his interest in Sophie, which might not have been the best idea, "I have a personal few things I'd like clear up."

Olivia nodded with understanding. "I'm still glad you came tonight. It's my first ever matchmaking set up, so I was pretty nervous. You made the nerves go away before the first inning was over, so thank-you for that."

"I hope it wasn't because I knocked you over," he laughed.

"Well, it took the awkwardness out of the introductions, that's for sure."

Before parting ways, Logan gave Olivia a piece of advice. "Don't be nervous for your next date. Sophie's good at this sort of thing." And with a wink, he walked to the parking lot.

Nine

Logan stomped his boots outside on the porch to get rid of as much mud as he could. Of course, it had to be Thursday evening, the night of his date with Sophie, that Eighty-four became ill. Mike had found the calf panting in the shade early in the afternoon, and both of them had been tending to her since. It was quarter to seven now, and he was fifteen minutes late for his date with Sophie. And filthy.

He had known the situation was going to take a while when the calf tried to run or escape every time they had touched her, so Logan had texted Sophie an hour ago telling her to let herself in since he would be a late. From the pasture, Logan had seen her car pull up the driveway only ten minutes ago.

He stripped his filthy jacket off and tossed it into the washing machine on his way by. There was no way he would wear that again without washing it given what he had been lying in for the past couple of hours. As he stepped into the hallway that led to the kitchen, Logan heard the faint sounds of the television. When he reached the living room, Sophie sat with her back to him on his leather recliner watching Jeopardy—answering almost every question correctly. Aloud.

She obviously hadn't heard him come in, so Logan listened to the next question without alerting her that he was there.

"This term describes the event when a defensive lineman tackles the quarterback before he throws or hands off the football," Alex, the host, read.

"What is a sack," Sophie and Logan said in unison.

Sophie whirled around at the sound of his voice clutching her chest. "You scared me," she growled playfully.

They both laughed while missing the rest of the category. "You're a pretty smart cookie," he said.

"Anna and I keep score whenever we watch it together."

"Oh, yeah? Who wins?"

Sophie shrugged. "Fifty-fifty."

"I know I would lose against you two. I caught a lucky break with that one," he motioned to the television as he took a step backwards towards the bathroom. "I'm going to take a quick shower because I know that what I'm covered in is *not* a smell I like to mix with food. I'll be out before final jeopardy."

Sophie was already waving him off as she paid attention to the next answer.

As Logan washed up and pulled on some clean clothes, he thought about how beautiful Sophie looked. She had left her hair loose around her shoulders and had worn a plain t-shirt and a comfortable pair of jeans. He liked that she hadn't applied layers of makeup or worn finicky clothing just to impress him. He wanted Sophie to be herself around him. He didn't want her to change a thing.

Since his set up with Olivia the other night, Logan had been in a great mood. Yes, he had had a good time at the baseball game, but a lot of that had to do with counting down the hours until his date tonight. This was the one that counted. Even Mike had asked him yesterday why he was acting weird. Logan had laughed at his statement implying that his happy mood was weird. He would have to work on that. When he told Mike about his upcoming night with Sophie, Mike had patted him on the back on his way out of the barn and muttered, "Don't screw this one up."

The remark had made Logan a little nervous because this really was the first time he really didn't want to mess it up. The nerves had faded when Logan remembered that conversation came easy between Sophie and him. They didn't have to push the small talk or pretend to be anything they weren't.

In the last few days, Logan had picked up his guitar again. The instrument used to bring mostly bad memories, so when he did decide to play it was always because he was in a good mood. It would push away the negativity that normally weighed him down while he strummed or sang. By being around Sophie lately, Logan's mood was the best it had been in a long time, and just last night, he composed a catchy melody line for some lyrics he had written almost a year ago. If this date went well tonight, he was sure it would lead to more lyrics, chords, and melodies.

It took him only a few minutes to dress in some clean jeans and a t-shirt and put a hat on over top of his hair that needed a trim. She was dressed comfortably, so he would too. On his way down the hallway to the kitchen and living room, Logan noticed his music room's door was ajar. Had he left it like that? No one except his father knew about his secret hobby, and he wasn't sure if he was ready to share it with Sophie. Maybe one day soon. He shrugged off the eerie feeling and went to get the date started.

He walked into the living room just as Jeopardy went to commercial.

"What's the category?"

"Canadian Islands."

"We might have a shot. I'll get dinner started." Once he had the barbeque lit on the deck just off his kitchen, Logan opened the refrigerator and took out steaks and some corn on the cob. He put them on the island to prep everything for the barbeque.

"Anything I can do to help?" Sophie asked.

"You can have a seat on one of those stools and keep me company."

She smiled at his teasing tone. "If you insist."

"I do. I think with the amount of work it took just to nail down tonight, I need to really impress you, so it's easier for next time," he said with a wink.

"I have a policy. If you feed me, I'll come back."

He laughed. "Consider yourself well fed for the foreseeable future."

Their easy banter continued while Logan put the steaks and corn on the barbeque and whipped up a Caesar salad to go with the meal. He had never had a date like this. Easy. Usually, he was trying to change the topic of conversation away from him settling down or raising children, and often, he was always checking his watch to see if it was time to end the evening. It left Logan questioning why he had done that to himself in the first place. Did he need the company that bad? Was that better than enjoying spending time with a friend who was a woman?

It seemed he had been wrong for almost a decade. Not all women were like the one he grew up around. Some did possess a sense of loyalty and kindness. With Sophie, conversation ranged from their likes and dislikes of food to exchanging childhood memories on their families' farms. She talked about Anna and the upcoming wedding from a woman's perspective, while he offered some insight from a man's point of view—lace and flowers versus seeing the bride for the first time and eating good food.

While they ate dinner on his back deck facing the evening's sunset, Logan even considered that maybe some day soon he might be willing to broach the conversational topics he had always avoided. He doubted, however, that he would ever be ready to talk openly about his mother's abandonment and disloyalty to the people she was supposed to love and care for. But with this new-found friendship with potential to develop into something more with Sophie, Logan was prepared to take baby steps in a direction he had never gone before.

Once dinner was cleaned up, Logan and Sophie returned to the back deck where Logan brought two patio chairs together so they were side by side. The horizon was painted with brilliant oranges and reds as the sun sank even lower. It was so peaceful to watch that they both sat in silence just gazing at the sky. At one point, Logan felt that he could share in the evening with Sophie just a little more, so he reached for her hand.

They sat just like that for almost an hour, hands joined and completely comfortable being in each other's company without the need for words. In all the years he worked in quiet pastures doing what he loved, Logan couldn't remember a time where he felt so at peace.

When a chill took its place in the evening air, Sophie finally broke the silence.

"It's late."

Logan checked his watch and noted it was later than he expected. It was just past nine o'clock. June's long days make the evenings longer as the sun would barely set before rising again.

"I'll walk you out," he said.

With their hands still linked, Logan led her through the house and down the front steps to her car. "Let's plan for another evening like this one. I'll feed you again," he said.

She giggled at his reference to their earlier joke. "Sunday."

"Let's have a picnic," he suggested.

Sophie smiled up at him, her eyes catching the light from his porch. "I'd like that."

"Sunday then."

With that, Sophie drove off. And Logan decided that was the best date he had ever had. Sunday couldn't come soon enough.

SOPHIE laid in bed staring out the window at the stars. She had watched them come out over an hour ago, which meant she had been laying there for almost two unable to sleep. It was official. She had a crush on Logan Fraser, cattle rancher with a mysterious musical hobby and an elusive past. And he was a non-believer. How had she wound up in this situation?

She laughed to herself. It had been her own doing—charmed by the tall, dark, and handsome. One thing was for sure though; she had gained a great friend. Their conversation had been easy, and she hadn't wanted the night to end as they sat facing the sunset with her hand in his in comfortable silence.

The evening had started off a bit strange when Sophie had given herself a tour of Logan's home while he was cleaning up before dinner. The door to the second bedroom had been open, so she had gone in to take a look. What she found was not at all what she expected. Instead of an extra bed with basic furniture to accommodate a guest or two, Sophie had found a variety of instruments—a keyboard, two acoustic guitars, and a bass guitar—with sheet music scattered on music stands and even on the floor. Some were hand written, some were chords and lyrics of popular songs she had heard on the radio.

And the photograph. On the far wall was a dusty shelf, and on it had been what looked like a family portrait. Logan stood between his parents holding a guitar. His father only had eyes for his mother, while Logan's mom gazed down at her son. She was beautiful. Long, straight hair hung down her sides, and her outfit showcasing what had to be the latest trends of that year fit to perfection. But what Sophie remembered most about the picture was that Logan's mother looked familiar. She just couldn't remember where she would have seen the woman.

Sophie dismissed the photograph and escaped the room feeling as if she had invaded Logan's privacy by accident. She decided that minute that if he wanted to disclose his hobby or talk about the photograph, he should be the one to bring up the subject.

Their conversation earlier gave Sophie limited information about Logan's family, but she decided not to push. It didn't mean she didn't have questions though. What had become of Mrs. Fraser? From what she could guess based on Logan's avoidance of the topic, his mother hadn't passed away, which meant something had pulled his family apart. Something big and drastic must have occurred in order for the family in that portrait to denounce their love for each other, because the way Lincoln looked at the woman and the way the woman looked at Logan indicated a strong bond between all three of them.

Sophie turned away from the window in an effort to push the thoughts away. As she drifted asleep, Sophie came to the conclusion that if she wanted a chance to talk about Jesus with Logan, the way to his heart was through his past and getting there would take time, patience, and prayer.

$\mathcal{T}_{en}$

Logan bounced along the gravel road in the direction of Sethburn. The clock on his dashboard claimed he would arrive at Sophie's right on time. The gorgeous Sunday weather did little to brighten his mood, however, because today would be the first time in a little over six months that he would attend church.

His phone conversation with Sophie yesterday had been a little awkward when she proposed the idea of heading to church and following it up with a picnic lunch. He hadn't known what to say. It was clear to any regular church attendee in Sethburn, since there was only one, that Logan was absent except for the odd holiday service Lincoln asked him to, which left him wondering why Sophie would ask him. It also made him nervous.

There was a good reason that Logan didn't go to church anymore. A week after his mother left him and his father, Logan abandoned the faith that he grew up with. If God allowed terrible things to happen to his family, then what kind of a God was

He? Not a loving one, and not one Logan wanted to pray to or worship or trust. He had lost a lot of friends after giving up on Jesus, but Logan never considered that as big of a letdown as the day his mother stepped out of the house and never looked back.

And now here he was—ready to brave a service for someone other than his father. He almost laughed at the thought. For a decade, he had purposely avoided this part of his past, and now that he had a little crush, he was willing to try it out. Even though he had no intention of letting Jesus back into his life, Logan decided he was willing to sit through an hour of songs and speeches for extra time with Sophie. So that was something.

After his phone call last night, he told Lincoln he would see him tomorrow morning. The look on his father's face was one he wasn't likely to forget. It was the second reason he was in his truck driving to town this morning. There had been an understanding between the two of them for years about Logan's church attendance and his lack of faith. Lincoln had promised a seventeen-year-old Logan that he would never force him to church, but he would pray from him every day. As a teenager, Logan was satisfied not having to talk about it anymore. But still, Logan never missed his father's disappointment when it came to his son abandoning his faith.

Last night had been different. When Logan mentioned that he would see him in church, Lincoln smiled wide. It was the most genuine grin Logan had seen from his father in many years. It was the same smile he wore in the only family photograph Logan had in his house. The one on the dusty shelf in his music room. It was the smile Lincoln wore when staring at his wife.

So today, he was hitting two birds with one stone. His dad would be pleased to see him there, and afterwards, he had a date with a beautiful girl.

He pulled into Sophie's driveway in front of her garage apartment and sent her a quick text message telling her he was there. Not even a minute passed when Sophie appeared from around the back wearing a floral summer dress and bright yellow flip-flops that matched her golden hair.

Today was going to be a good day.

THEY still had a few minutes before needing to find a seat in the sanctuary. Sophie had gotten sidetracked chatting with Mrs. Lloyd about her 'very single' nephew, while Logan waited patiently at her side to finish up and find a seat. As she said a quick good-bye, Logan reached for her hand to lead her inside.

His grip was warm and firm, and it felt nice. But Sophie felt the odd sensation that she was being rushed. She could only guess that Logan might be uncomfortable being in church this morning given his sporadic previous attendance and what she could only guess as a difficult event from his past, but now, with her hand in his, she was grateful that he accepted her invitation.

Just as they found an empty row, Lincoln stopped them before sitting down.

"Good morning, you two," he greeted with dancing eyes and large grin.

"Mr. Fraser. I see you've got your nametag on. Usher duty today?" she asked.

"You bet. I'll let you two get to your seat." He pulled Sophie into a hug before whispering, "Thank-you, dear. You have no idea how much I've been praying to see my son here." And with that, he went back to his place at the door to greet more of the morning's congregation, but not before he welcomed his son into the house of the Lord with a hearty pat on the back.

Sophie was glad to know that Lincoln prayed for his son as diligently as she did—probably more so, but given Logan's current state, she kept her thoughts to herself as the piano player began an introduction to the service's first worship song. *Called Me Higher* by All Sons & Daughters was one of her favourites. The lyrics always spoke to her in a special way, just as they did this morning. She leaned her hands on the pew in front of her and closed her eyes, allowing the melody and lyrics to wash over her.

I could be safe, I could be safe here in Your arms and never leave home,
Never let these walls down.
But You have called me higher, You have called me deeper,
I'll go where You will lead me Lord.

This was the reason Sophie started her business. It was a way to step out of the comfort of everyday life and do something that pleased God. His plans for Sophie didn't include working nine to five at the post office waiting for life to start—no, His plans for her involved outreach, community, and love. Love, above everything else.

The message that followed the worship from Pastor Tim was on that very subject. He emphasized how difficult it is to understand God's love and how vast and unconditional it is at all times. The scripture passage for the morning came from Ephesians:

I pray that you, being rooted and established in love, may have power, together with all the Lord's holy people, to grasp how wide and long and high and deep is the love of Christ.

The words hit Sophie square in the chest. The passage would serve as the perfect mission statement for Match 'Em Up because her ultimate goal was to have couples grow to love each other with God's love as an example. She reached to her side for her purse where she kept a notebook for moments like this only to find Logan's hand instead of her bag. In that split second, grasping his hand served a greater purpose than a pen and paper ever would. That verse and that moment would forever create a beautiful memory—creating a connection with help from God.

She could feel it, and she hoped with everything in her that he could too.

As the service came to a close, Sophie bowed her head and prayed for the friend beside her. *Lord, be with Logan in a special way this morning. Let him feel Your comfortable and steady presence, a presence he can lean on with whatever burden he is carrying. Bless his day with reminders of You and the wide, long, high, deep, unconditional love You have for Him. Amen.*

With their hands still linked, Logan led Sophie from the church after the service had ended. He stayed quiet as they got into the truck and drove away, and Sophie just knew something special was happening inside of him. She couldn't wait to see what God had in store for both of them.

The park they decided on the night before was the same one where Logan watched the baseball game just days before. The area took up almost the entire west side of Sethburn with a soccer pitch, two ball diamonds, a large playground, and a grassy area with picnic tables and horseshoe pits. The park was well maintained by a few town workers, but mostly, volunteers cared for the park by mowing lawns, raking sand, painting fences, dugouts, and playground equipment. In fact, Sophie recalled that even when she was in high school students would volunteer their time at the park in exchange for baseball and soccer equipment to use there.

When they pulled into the gravel parking lot in front of the picnic area, they could see the tables already filling up with families. It was the perfect day—the sun was bright, only a few clouds scattering the sky, and the soft breeze was just enough to take the edge off the summer heat. Logan reached for the cooler in the box of his truck while tucking a blanket under one arm, and they made their way to an empty spot on the grass. They chose a spot where a tree provided just enough shade to ward off sunburn, which Sophie appreciated given her pale complexion.

"Right here is perfect," she announced.

Logan smiled back at her. "I think so, too."

Once the blanket was spread out, Sophie removed her shoes and sat down. Logan had worn sneakers and socks, so he opted to keep his on.

"I love the feeling of grass running through my toes and under my feet," she explained. "It's the quickest way for me to relax—feels like a little slice of heaven."

"Do you like running your toes through the snow too?" Logan joked. "Because that makes up the other half of the year."

Sophie gave him a gentle shove. "If you must know, I have this old shag area rug beside my bed. It feels almost exactly like grass, so I make do with that during the winter."

"I'm glad because if the feeling of grass between your toes makes you smile, you should get to feel it every day." His sincere smile and his genuine words gave her butterflies. The good kind, the anticipatory kind. And she welcomed that feeling too.

LOGAN laid out the food from the cooler—two BLT sandwiches, slices of melon, some grapes, a bag of Lays potato chips, and two bottles of water.

"Wow, this looks great. Thanks for making lunch, I'm starved."

"Kept it simple," he said, ignoring thoughts about his mild moment of panic last night deciding on a picnic lunch menu. He had no idea what was typical—he hadn't packed a lot of picnics in his day. The closest thing to it had been when he packed food for a daylong deer hunting trip, and that had consisted of granola bars, a Gatorade, and two apples. He had eaten it all before noon rolled around and had gone hungry for the rest of the day. He guessed sandwiches were better than granola bars and simple enough for him to make.

He divided the sandwiches between two paper plates along with the chips and handed her a bottle of water.

"Would you mind if I said grace?"

Her question caught him off guard, but he did his best not to show it by shuffling his napkin around to look busy rather than uncomfortable. "Uh, sure."

She grabbed his hand in what he assumed was a routine gesture before praying for the meal. "God, we just want to thank You for this beautiful day—the gorgeous sunshine, the serene park with grass we can sink our toes into," she giggled before continuing, "and for the opportunity to spend this morning looking into Your word to understand a little bit more of how vast Your love is for us. Please bless this afternoon, bless this wonderful lunch, and bless Logan for preparing it. Amen."

She released his hand and reached for her sandwich, and he didn't know quite what to think. His dad still prayed before a meal, so the concept wasn't foreign to him, but it had been a while since he heard anybody pray for him specifically. But what shocked him most is that he appreciated her thoughtfulness. He didn't feel resentment, he didn't feel uncomfortable, he didn't feel anything but humbled that Sophie thought of him during her quick conversation with God.

He cleared his throat in an effort to regain some composure. "Uh, thanks."

She covered her mouth full of food, but still replied with a muffled "your welcome" and a smile.

They ate in comfortable silence taking in the park and the people. Off to the side two young boys played an unsuccessful game of catch with a Frisbee while their parents looked on. They fumbled the disc on every throw but didn't lose heart to keep at it. Logan loved children; in fact, he couldn't wait for hockey season to begin. He and Drake had already signed up again to coach the peewee team in the fall. It would be their third year in a row.

Logan didn't often think about having children of his own one day because he was always uninterested in having a long-term relationship with any woman. But now he found himself thinking of what it would be like to coach his own son or daughter on the ice one day. Teaching them to wrestle a calf, brand cattle, saddle a horse. He smiled at the thought.

"That looks like so much fun," Sophie said as she packed up her empty plate after sweeping her crumbs onto the grass.

"Frisbee?" he asked.

"Yes, I wish I had the knack for it."

She watched the boys with a wistfulness that had Logan saying, "I'll teach you."

"Now?" she asked as she turned his way.

He laughed. "Nah, I don't think they like it much if we stole their toy. I've got one at home. It's all in the flick of the wrist." He demonstrated with an imaginary disc a couple of times.

"Looks complicated."

"Nah, I've got faith in you."

They packed up what was left of their lunch into the cooler and Sophie tossed the rest in a garbage can nearby while Logan folded up the blanket.

He held her hand all the way back to the truck and decided that it was his new favourite thing to do. It felt right, her small hand engulfed in his.

He drove toward her place—her and Anna had a few wedding details to see to tonight. Sophie reached for the radio and tuned it to the country music station. Three words into the song, Logan froze.

He had heard those lyrics a thousand times, but never through a speaker. No, he heard the song from the lips of his mother. He heard it the first time she uttered the first line, when she composed the melody line, when she fine-tuned the harmonies, when she sang it at the top of her lungs after her manager called with news of a record deal.

Logan hated this song.

His knuckles blanched as he gripped the steering wheel as tight as he could. Coming off such a great afternoon with Sophie, he didn't want to ruin it now, so he asked as politely as he could, "Mind if I switch the station?"

"Sure—," Sophie looked his way, "Are you alright? You face is a little red."

He waved her off as he flicked to the nearest station—pop music, fine. Anything else was better.

"Probably just the sun," he deflected.

"Hmm, we should remember sunscreen next time."

If only the solution was that simple.

Eleven

Sophie stared out of her office window onto Main Street. She hadn't accomplished a single thing in the hour she had been at work this morning. She was too caught up in reliving her time with Logan on Sunday. Yesterday she had been busy with client meetings and phone calls hearing about how dates went over the weekend, but now, with a few spare minutes, Sophie was daydreaming.

The day had given her a lot of insight into some of the more mysterious sides of Logan. She learned little about his fun-loving nature, because she was already familiar with that part of him—she decided it was one of the many reasons her crush had developed into a serious case of like. But she learned much more about the state of his faith. And the only part that she had found comforting was that he agreed to come to church with her.

He had obviously been uncomfortable throughout the whole thing, silent during the worship, squirming during the message.

What she still did not understand was why his father's strong Christian beliefs hadn't rubbed off on his son. Sophie could only guess that it had a lot to do with that family portrait she found in Logan's house and the lack of information about his mother.

She predicted that his closed off behaviour as he dropped her off also had a great deal to do with his childhood. It was clear Logan had a lot to think about, and some of those heavy subjects were weighing on his mind even during their date. It was a good thing though—Logan needed to work out all those things before their relationship could really bloom.

So she would be patient.

But one thing she knew for sure—Logan was not at all like the reputation he had been given. Who people thought of as a ladies' man with commitment issues, was really a kind hearted, deep thinking, loyal, caring man.

Sophie pulled herself from the daydreaming and shuffled some papers around her desk. Constantly thinking about Logan would not make the situation any better. She would just have to take it one day at a time. Checking her calendar, Sophie noticed that she had a few client calls to make informing them of new matches and scheduled dates.

An hour later she only had one call left to make. It was a call she wanted to make, but didn't want to talk about business. But this was her job, and they had made a silly agreement.

He answered after three rings. "Logan here."

"Hi, it's Sophie." She heard hammering in the background even as Logan grew further from the noise. "Is this a good time?"

"Fine time, actually. I could use a break."

The hammering continued but much quieter. "You're not going to like the reason I'm calling," she said with a little humour and a bit of dread.

"Is there good news first? I like my good news first," he teased.

She laughed appreciating how he made the situation lighter. "Okay. Good news is I make a mean coffee cake." It was the first thing that came to her mind when he put her on the spot like that.

"Mmm, that is good news. What's the bad?"

"You have a date tomorrow night," she rushed. Now, she would really have to make him one of those coffee cakes.

There was a pause before he said, "Which I am going to assume is not with you or you would have started with that instead of teasing me with your baking skills."

"Treat it as more of a citizen of Sethburn welcoming a new-comer. Amy just moved here—actually, to Shell Lake—and since she was a match, I figured it would alright if you showed her around some."

"So it's not a date?" He sounded confused.

"It is because it will officially be your last one as a client of Match 'Em Up, but it'll be as if you're just showing her around."

"I can do that. Last one though, right?"

She smiled at his insistence and thought again of how wrong his reputation was. "Right."

"Okay. Hit me with some details, I want to get this over with."

LOGAN ended the call from Sophie and laughed a little. By tomorrow evening all the riff raff and hoopla of a three date contract with a matchmaker would be over, and then he could focus on pursuing that very matchmaker. No more dates with women—it turned out they weren't so bad—who weren't the one he had his heart set on. He decided to plan something special, a night to be remembered as he and Sophie would make it official. Or, that was his plan anyway. Maybe Mike would have some ideas.

Logan sauntered over to the new calf shoot they were assembling not in a hurry to get back to the tiring work.

"Mike, what do you say it's time for a break?" he shouted over the pounding.

Mike poked his head up and looked around for Logan. "Sounds good to me. I need a refill," he said gesturing for his water bottle.

Once they settled themselves against some sawhorses with cold water, Logan decided to come right out with it. "Got any good date ideas?"

Mike choked on the last sip. "Come again?" he asked between coughing.

Suddenly, Logan felt a little shy about the whole situation. "I, uh—I want to plan something cool, something special I guess for our next date."

Logan could tell his friend was trying to hold back a laugh. "And you thought to ask me? What do I know?"

Logan was growing more embarrassed. He had never been this guy—the one who fusses over a woman, plans special dates. "Just forget it, man. Forget I asked—"

"Hey, now. I appreciate you asking though. Just wish I could help you out."

Logan chuckled at Mike's obvious lack of sincerity. "Yeah, whatever."

As they made their way back over to the calf shoot, Mike asked, "I thought you already did something special. Sunday, I thought. Lincoln mentioned something on Friday that you had plans."

"Are you gonna laugh at me if I tell you about it?" Logan asked while playfully shoving Mike's arm.

"No, man. Tell me."

While they assembled more of the new shoot, Logan did exactly that. He gave Mike a summary of the events—church, the picnic in the park, giving a little more detail about his lack of picnic packing skills that Sophie didn't seem to notice. He told him about the tentative plan to teach her how to play Frisbee and how he was glad she was a girl who wasn't afraid to be outside, get her hands dirty with sports or other things.

"Sounds like you had a good time."

Logan nodded. "Yeah, that's why I asked for ideas. I have a lot to live up to now."

They laughed as Mike said, "Sorry I'm no help with that."

They worked in silence for the next few minutes, lifting and attaching heavy piece after heavy piece. Once the last of it was fit in place, Logan lifted his hat to swipe the sweat from his forehead.

Just as he placed his hat back on, Mike asked, "What did you think of church?"

The question caught Logan off guard. In fact, since Sunday Logan had pushed that topic from his mind, unwilling to think about how it felt to sit in a pew, and listen to the pastor talk about the very God that let him down.

Sunday evening after dropping Sophie off at her home, Logan had been a sour mood. Not from his time with her—definitely not the time he spent with that beautiful girl, but his mood had stemmed from his struggle to listen to someone preach about unconditional love, deep, wide, high, all-encompassing love. And not to mention the coincidence of his mother's greatest hit playing on the radio that afternoon. It was as if his past had hit him head on. How could a God with such great love allow his mother to dispense of her family in trade for fame? No matter how he spun it, Logan could never justify why God let that happen to him or to his father.

"It was, uh, just like all the other times I've been there. Why do you ask?"

"I'd like to go sometime. I haven't been for a little while, and I miss it."

Logan was taken aback. He had no idea his ranch hand was a believer. In fact, in all the time Mike had worked for him, never once had he mentioned church or God.

"You're a Christian?" Logan asked.

Mike cleared his throat as if he were a little nervous. "Uh, yeah. It's new though."

Logan didn't know what to say and was given a reprieve as Mike's cell phone rang right then.

"Mike here." Logan watched as his eyes grew wide. "Well, is he alright? Okay, good. Should I drive over? Are you sure? I'll call tonight to talk to him just like I always do. Yeah, okay, see you Friday. 'Bye." He closed the phone and put it in his pocket looking somewhat dazed.

"Everything okay?" Logan asked.

Mike lifted his hat and scratched his head while he found his words. "Uh, I guess. My son fell down the stairs."

Logan reeled at the news, but tried not to let it show. "Did you say you have a son?"

Mike looked up again with a surprised expression. Logan instantly knew he hadn't meant to reveal that piece of information. "I did."

"He's okay?" Logan asked again getting some wits about him now.

"Yeah, yeah. Cut his forehead on the banister on his way down. He's got a bandage and a black eye, but she said he'll be okay." Mike leaned against the calf shoot for support and reached for a water bottle.

"What's his name?"

"Caiden. He's awesome. Actually, he's the best."

"Is this where you've been going every weekend lately?" Logan didn't want to pry, but Mike's admission was information that was hard to ignore.

Mike smiled. "Yeah."

"You got a woman that comes with your boy?"

Mike's expression changed to one of sadness as he nodded. "Lives with his mom. She's pretty great too, but she's not mine."

"She anybody else's?" With Mike's quipped answers, Logan felt like he wasn't getting anywhere close to understanding his ranch hand's complicated family.

"No."

Logan laughed before he said, "And I thought asking you for date suggestions was a good idea."

Mike's grin came back as Logan walked away glad he could lighten the mood again. "Let me know if you need some time off. It's yours for the taking," he called back.

As he reached the house, Logan came to one conclusion. His friend was a good man who stood by his child even when the situation was tough. It was a lot more than what he could say about his own parent.

"I'M so sorry I'm late," the petite brunette that sat down across from him said.

Logan assumed this was Amy—his 'date' for the evening. Sophie had set up the date so they would meet at the park. Logan picked up some pancakes to-go from Earl and had arrived five minutes early to grab a picnic table for them both.

"No problem. I'm Logan." He stuck out his hand for her to shake.

She grabbed it and gave two quick pumps before releasing it and eyeing the paper bags with their meal. "The sitter was late, therefore, I'm late," she said as another apology.

He was intrigued. "Sibling or child?"

Amy smiled. "Child. He's six."

"Very cool." He dished out their dinner dividing the stack of pancakes and sausages almost evenly, giving himself an extra pancake. Just as Logan dug into his first bite, Amy bowed her head for a few moments. He was a little embarrassed, but she didn't seem fazed. He decided to act as if it never happened and took a bite. "Sophie says I should play tour guide tonight."

"That would be great, actually. I'm new to the area. I moved to Shell Lake a few months ago to be closer to family. I haven't been out much yet."

Logan smiled. "You'll be an expert of Sethburn by the end of tonight."

They finished their food without speaking, both just enjoying breakfast for dinner. Then Logan walked Amy around the small town. They started with the City Hall, which was really just an addition built on to the side of the recreation center. Logan explained that he coached the peewee hockey team.

"Your son should join the team in fall. It's a great way to get to know people in the community. He'll be just the right age."

Amy considered the idea, but was worried how he would do on skates. He had only ice-skated twice before, but she promised to keep it in mind.

They moved down Main Street passing the post office, the florist, and the hardware store. Logan talked about each of the business owners, and Amy kept interrupting asking how he knew all of the people. He shrugged and blamed it on the typical small town mentality. Finally, they passed Sophie's office, which Amy hadn't seen yet since she had filled out an application at a mixer a few months ago.

"She's so nice. Sophie has been nothing but helpful in my silly quest to meet new people around here," Amy said staring at Match 'Em Up's storefront.

"She really is the best, isn't she?" Logan said with absolutely no shame.

Amy caught on to his statement right away, and asked him, "Wouldn't dating a matchmaker be complicated?"

Logan laughed outright. "You have no idea."

They turned around to head back to their vehicles. Almost half way back to the park, Amy's phone rang.

"It's the sitter, I've got to answer this," she explained before answering. "Josie, is everything okay? Uh huh. Right, well just make him an extra-large glass of chocolate milk and explain that if that pill isn't swallowed by the time I get home he'll be helping me clean the house on Saturday. Okay, bye."

Logan chuckled as Amy's pace picked up after ending the call. "Are we in a hurry now?"

"A little. He hurt himself just yesterday and the doctor gave him some pills to help with his headache before he goes to bed. You know, something stronger than kids' Tylenol but still safe for his age? He doesn't like to swallow them."

"Then by all means, let's hurry back."

They said a quick goodbye at their vehicles before Amy sped off in the direction of Shell Lake.

Logan pulled out his phone before driving out of the parking lot. He typed Sophie a quick message. *Bad news—I don't have a future in tour guiding. Good news—future dates will be with this really special girl who apparently makes a mean coffee cake. She has yet to prove it though.*

Twelve

Logan did a final check through his house. It had been a few weeks since he was able to give it a good clean, and the afternoon before a date with Sophie seemed like a good time. He had chicken marinating in the refrigerator, a salad ready to be dressed, and some corn on the cob waiting to be grilled. His iPod played some country hits quietly in its dock. The forecast predicted some rain late in the evening, so Logan had set the table inside for dinner.

Now, he had fifteen minutes to wait.

Tonight Logan wanted to make things official with Sophie. He wanted a label on their relationship, a real commitment—no more silly deals or scheduling day to day. He wanted to give a real relationship a try for the first time, but only with Sophie.

He couldn't remember ever being this nervous before. Not even his first day of school after he and Lincoln had moved to Sethburn had been this nerve-racking. And since his anxiety was getting the best of him, he couldn't help but wonder if she would say no. What would happen then?

This morning came to mind when Mike had cornered him in the shop. Logan had been a total klutz this morning forgetting tools and dropping parts just thinking about what he was going to say to Sophie tonight, and Mike had to make sure he was alright.

Logan quietly admitted to being a bit anxious about tonight, and Mike's reply had been, "I may not be the best person to ask for dating advice, but maybe I can help calm the nerves. When you go in for lunch, check out Jeremiah 29:11. It helps me calm down whenever I worry."

Logan hadn't said anything in reply to Mike's advice and instead, did as he asked on his lunch break.

'For I know the plans I have for you,' declares the Lord, 'plans to prosper you and not to harm you, plans to give you hope and a future.'

Logan remembered the verse from many years of Sunday school when he was a child. He had memorized it several times earning stickers and high-fives as prizes. But never once had Logan pondered the context.

He wasn't quite sure how Mike thought it was applicable for tonight, but he'd keep it mind. He appreciated the encouragement of the verse—a promise for a brighter future—but he had to get Sophie to agree to one with him first.

As he waited out the last few minutes before Sophie's arrival, Logan was struck by an alarming thought. In the past week the topic of God had come up more times that in had in the last year, and not once did he get a consuming feeling of disgust but instead a feeling of anxiousness. What was that about?

Logan wasn't given time to ponder the question when he spotted Sophie's car come up his driveway leaving a cloud of dust in its wake.

He welcomed her at the door with a glass of iced tea and ushered her in.

"Figured we'd eat inside instead of taking our chances with the forecast," he said while helping her out of her jacket.

"Sounds good to me. I'm having a good hair day and don't want to wreck it with the wind," she teased.

Logan inspected her hair pretending to examine it mimicking what he thought a hairstylist might do. After a moment he said, "I can't tell the difference. It looks good every day."

Sophie laughed. "Typical."

Logan mock gasped. "Did you just label me with a stereotype?"

In between chuckles, she added, "I totally did."

"No fair. My assessment was accurate."

"Well then, my gratitude is in order."

Logan directed her to the table. "Good. Save it for when you've tasted the meal."

Thirty minutes later, the chicken and corn were grilled and the salad was dressed. Sophie kept him company while he manned the barbeque. Just as he slid the patio door closed the first raindrop hit the deck.

Perfect timing.

Normally when Logan made himself a meal, he sat on his recliner with a TV tray over his lap while watching whatever sports game was on. Today was different. Once all the food was on the table, Logan asked Sophie if she'd say grace. He was definitely not comfortable enough to be doing that himself, but he respected her need to do it.

She hesitated only a second before giving him a nod and a smile. "Sure."

Logan watched as she bowed her head and began. "God, thank You for today. Thanks for giving Logan and I this time together to enjoy each other's company. Thank You for blessing us with this wonderful meal and for Logan who prepared it. Bless our conversation this evening as well. In Your name, Amen."

The concept of blessing a meal was not foreign to Logan, but it had been awhile since he participated. Whenever he had dinner with his father, Lincoln would bow his head before the meal. But years ago, he had given up praying aloud when Logan made a fuss about it. Now, he didn't feel awkward at all because he respected Sophie and her decisions. Maybe Logan had some reevaluating to do the next time he sat down at a table with his father.

The chicken turned out just as he hoped. The marinade had sealed the moisture in and had given it a bit of a kick. The corn was salted and buttered just the way he liked, and Sophie seemed to enjoy the salad judging by the two helpings she had.

It was getting to be that time when Logan planned to bring up the status of their relationship and his nerves began to sink in. As he rinsed and loaded the plates into the dishwasher, the verse Mike had given him earlier came to mind. He still wasn't sure how it fit into tonight, but a sense of peace settled on his shoulders as his remembered the words. Now or never, he decided.

"Join me in the living room," he asked offering his hand to help her from the dining room chair. She took his hand as he led her to the leather loveseat that faced the living room window. From it, they could see an entire quarter section. Near the back of the pasture, cows and calves grazed, and closer to the house the barn casted shadows on the bales stacked along it. It was the view Logan enjoyed every morning with a cup of coffee.

"So I wanted to clear something up with you today," he began.

He sensed her nervousness at his change of topic, but carried on. "Now that I have reluctantly gone a three dates with three woman, none of whom I have an interest in dating again, and am no longer a client of yours, I wanted to know if you'd consider making it official. You and I." He cleared his throat, but didn't add anymore. He didn't want to ramble.

The few moments she stayed quiet were almost too much to bear. It was just long enough for doubt to creep in.

"Uh—wow," she started, "That's, umm. Logan, I am flattered." He sensed a 'but'.

"But—" here it was, "you know my faith is everything. I have always promised myself that whomever I'm with will share that with me. And I don't know if you're ready for that." She grabbed ahold of his hand, but he wasn't certain if it was to reassure him or herself judging by her grip.

"You're a great friend. Really. And I really do have a serious crush on you," they both smiled at her admission, and Logan let her continue, "but I have to be upfront with you. Are you ready for something like that?"

Logan let out a sigh. It wasn't a 'no', but it was close. This situation called for complete honesty, and that's what he would give her. "I don't know if I am. God and I have different opinions, that's for sure. He really let me down in my past. Truly, deeply, destroyed me to be precise. But lately— since being around you, actually—I've gotten a bit curious about the whole faith thing. It lost its appeal years ago for me, but my father, your family, Drake, even my ranch hand, seem to be holding on tight to the idea. It makes me wonder if I missed something big."

He couldn't believe he had opened up to her like this—telling her his secrets and his feelings about God. But it felt right, natural.

She squeezed his hand with hers. "I'm glad you're curious. That's a good start."

"You're not upset?" he blurted before he could stop himself. When he had played out the scenario of Sophie rejecting him because of his faith, he hadn't pictured this. It almost sounded as if there might be hope for the two of them yet.

"Of course not. Everyone's journey with God is different and never equal. Who am I to judge your spiritual life when I need to be busy working on mine? No one is perfect. It hurts knowing you struggled enough to leave God behind, and I hope one day that'll change. But for right now, I have a crush on a guy who's curious about God, and that makes me excited."

In that intimate moment, Logan and Sophie shared a smile. This woman had been under his nose for years, and he had no idea how special she really was. It was a miracle that they were together now, and Logan hoped she would wait around long enough to give them an honest chance.

They stayed quiet for a while just enjoying the view from the living room as raindrops glided down the window. They still held one another's hands—a simple gesture, but meaningful. It meant that in some way they were joined. Together.

"Maybe one day you'll tell me about it."

Sophie's whisper was barely loud enough to be heard over the sound of the rain, but Logan caught every word. And in their state of honesty, Logan decided there was no time like the present. He stood from the couch and tugged her hand motioning for her to do the same.

"Come with me."

SOPHIE was a step behind Logan as he led her into his music room. It was less dusty than the last time she had been in here on her self-guided tour. The guitar had been moved and new sheets of music sat on a stand.

Logan pulled her over to the only stool in the room. While she sat down, he reached for the photo she had seen weeks ago. He kept it in his hands as he sat down on the floor facing her. Sophie watched as Logan's mind went to another place, another time—a time, she could only guess, that wasn't pleasant. But she waited patiently for Logan to be ready to share.

It took a while. Minutes passed as Logan's thumb traced the faces in the photo, as his eyes shut and opened and shut and opened again as if he was fighting back tears. She waited as he searched for the right words. And there was nowhere else she would have rather been. She was being given an opportunity few had been granted.

He started quiet and spoke slowly, methodically. "From the time I could remember, my mom would tuck me in and sing to me every night. She never sang lullabies or hymns or Sunday school songs. No. Mom, she would sing her current favourite song on the radio. A rock song, a ballad, a country song, you name it she sung it and played along with a guitar sometimes if the mood struck her. I knew all of ABBA's greatest hits by the time I was six. And she was good." Logan paused and traced the faces with his thumb again. Seconds passed, and he took a deep breath before continuing. "The only problem was that she thought she was too good. Good enough that she should be noticed by someone other than her husband or her son. Good enough that singing in church was cuttin' it. Good enough that being content with singing the national anthem at school assemblies or singing in the living room while we all danced together wasn't an option any more. So she went and got noticed."

Logan's eyes were shut as he leaned against the wall. Sophie's heart began to break for the small boy inside of Logan that was telling her the story. The boy whose heart seemed to be breaking all over again.

"She told us she was going on a girls' weekend to a spa in Montana. Well, it was a girls' weekend in that my aunt drove her to the airport. Instead of Montana, Mom ended up in Nashville. It only took the weekend for her to find a band, an agent, and a manager. Turned out that Nashville loved her. So she came home that Sunday afternoon and spilled the beans to my father while I was doing some chores outside. I walked into the garage at ten that night from feeding cows to find my mother loading her suitcase in the back of her car."

Sophie moved off the stool to sit beside Logan, shoulder to shoulder, as she sensed the hardest words were coming. His breath hitched as she grabbed his hand to comfort him. She couldn't imagine what that would have been like. She watched her sister move away to Toronto for a career and that was tough, but it was nothing compared to someone's mother choosing fame over family.

"She didn't even try to explain. She didn't even say anything to me. My mom didn't even give me a hug. I watched as she backed out of the garage without even a second glance at her husband and her son."

"Sweetheart, I'm so sorry." Sophie began rubbing his back in a comforting motion, like one would use to calm a child.

"I waited two days for my father to gather enough words to tell me what was going on. By then he'd found this ranch, and right after he told me why mom left, he told me to pack my bags. You heard of that song 'Beaches and Bare Feet'?"

"Yeah." It had been the song Logan had abruptly shut off in his truck on their picnic date. It was catchy, and she hummed along to it every time she heard it on the radio.

"You know who sings it?"

Sophie swallowed the lump in her throat at the realization. She was the hottest act in country music for several years running, and now, Sophie would never look at her the same. "Stacy-Lynn Freemont is your mother."

"She was."

She wasn't surprised with Logan's use of past tense. With his head still leaned against the wall, Logan wiped at a tear that escaped down his cheek. They sat in stillness for a while. Sophie wasn't sure if Logan was finished with the story or if he needed time to gather himself, so the quiet dragged on as they sat side by side against the wall.

It was clear that Logan hadn't shared any of this with many people. In fact, she was almost certain Drake didn't even know the extent of it. She couldn't imagine how it would feel to live with the pain Logan felt everyday—to live with the knowledge that you weren't enough for your mother, that she chose a life that didn't include you. It made sense now why Logan was reluctant to seek Jesus when his childhood held so much hurt. It made even more sense to Sophie how much Logan needed Jesus in his life *today*. Jesus could take away his hurt, his pain, his anger and replace it with faith, hope, and love.

"Can I pray for you?" she asked in a whisper.

"Yeah." He didn't even hesitate with his answer.

Sophie reached her arm around Logan shoulders and held him close to her. "God, I just want to lift up Logan to You right now. I pray that You would shine Your light on him—take away the darkness he feels from his past and replace it with Your goodness. Lord, I ask that you would guide Logan away from the shadows that chase him and burden him, that You would show him the way out of this valley of darkness. God, I want to thank You for bringing him into my life, for blessing both of us with a growing friendship. And especially now, I ask that You would have Your hand in what becomes of our relationship—that it would honour You, Lord. Amen."

Logan reached for Sophie's hand that was still resting on his shoulder. "Thank you for listening. And for praying."

"Anytime. I mean it," she promised.

Logan stood and crossed the room to his neat corner of instruments. "I didn't intend for tonight to be so heavy. Actually, I wanted it to be the opposite of that," he huffed with a chuckle, bringing a lightness back to their conversation.

Sophie watched as Logan plucked the acoustic guitar from its stand and slung the strap over his shoulder. "I'm glad you told me."

"I'm glad too." His smile melted what was left of her emotions. "Can we go back to when I asked you to go steady?" he joked.

"Logan, I—" she started.

He waved off whatever she was going to say. "I know, I know. But I still want to impress you. That's what a guy's gotta do, right, to get the girl?" he teased.

Sophie understood the seriousness of the evening had passed, and Logan needed a breather. So she joined in the fun. "Alright. Impress me."

Seconds later the room was filled with a beautiful melody. Logan's nimble fingers danced across the strings as his picked string after to string creating a harmonious tune. Sophie watched him in his element—shoulders bent over the guitar, face relaxed, eyes closed, swaying with the rhythm of the song. And when she thought it couldn't get better than listening to Logan play the acoustic guitar, he began to sing.

If I could be the fire in your firefly,
The cool in the rain, the spark in your eye
The answer to your prayers and the faith that sets you free
Then I'd be what you mean to me

Sophie recognized the song almost right away. It was the same one they danced to at the mixer only a few short weeks ago. His fingers transitioned from picking the strings to soft strums as Logan played into the chorus. She memorized the last two lines.

If falling's how you feel and perfect's what you see

Then I'd be what you mean to me

Logan sang through the chorus once more and continued to play for a few minutes after that. It was, Sophie decided, one of the top three moments of her life. Number one was the day she accepted Jesus, number two was the day Anna moved back to Sethburn, and number three was this very minute.

The strumming slowed and Logan opened his eyes to look at her. "So?"

"Can you do me a favour?"

"Anything."

"Can you come sit back over here and play it again?"

His grin was the largest she'd ever seen it. Logan sat down beside her again, but before he started playing he leaned his forehead against hers. "Sophie—"

She understood the magnitude of the one word. The emotion, the relief, the anticipation. All of it. She felt it. "Me too."

His hand reached up to cup her chin, and his lips touched hers for just a moment. It was long enough that Sophie understood Logan's intentions to build their relationship from a friendship into something more, but short enough to know that those intentions included respecting her above everything else.

With their foreheads still resting again each other's, Sophie asked, "Will you sing it again?"

"Absolutely."

Thirteen

Sophie sat next to Logan in the pew and tried to pay attention to Pastor Tim. It was difficult given that she seemed to be floating on clouds since last night. The great conversation, the news that Logan was curious about God again, the sweet kiss—it had been one of the greatest times she could remember. And now sitting in church with her hand in Logan's, her mind kept wandering to yesterday.

With great effort, Sophie shoved aside her euphoric thoughts and focused on the message. It wouldn't be saying much if she encouraged Logan to come to church and didn't even pay attention herself.

The pastor was speaking from 1 Peter. He read the Scripture aloud before diving into the message. "Above all, love each other deeply because love covers over a multitude of sins."

He went on to explain that people often lose sight of the heart of a person because of one mistake. That one action could hurt too deeply that sometimes it could become too difficult to overlook their wrongdoing and see the person past their mistakes. That was the moment to call on God for help. He could see through everyone's faults straight to their soul. He could see the good and beautiful person under their sin and love them unconditionally.

Sophie thought of just last year when Anna was living in Toronto with almost no connection to their family—minimal phone calls, Christmas cards, a Facebook message here and there. Sophie could have chosen to get angry, granted she had those days occasionally, but she looked to God instead. She prayed for Anna everyday, prayed that she would seek out the relationship with God she once had. She loved her sister despite the distance and lack of communication. And God had answered her prayers. Not only did Anna move back to Sethburn, but also rebuilt relationships with their parents, Sophie, and was now engaged to Drake, her childhood best friend. Anna sat only a small distance down the same pew with Drake's arm draped over her shoulders.

It was tough for Sophie to love her sister unconditionally when she didn't agree with Anna's choices, but she was glad she did. Sophie's sisterly love that only God helped her show had played a part in Anna's return home.

Sophie decided she would need to do the same thing with Logan. Love him, as a friend for now, unconditionally, so that maybe he would catch a glimpse of God's love for him. She could only hope that one day Logan would be able to love his mother again and overlook those sins. The burden he was carrying was too heavy; he wouldn't last much longer without dealing with those feelings before it would be too much. She didn't want to consider what the fallout would be if he kept shouldering the anger from his childhood.

Pastor Tim began his closing prayer bringing Sophie back to the present. She had missed that last half of the message, but the scripture from 1 Peter would stick with her for quite some time, she was sure of it.

Logan and her chatted casually with Anna and Drake as they filtered out of the sanctuary. Drake and Anna made afternoon plans to build a small gazebo for their wedding photos, so Logan and Sophie decided to head to Flatlands for some breakfast for lunch.

They rode together in Logan's truck since he'd picked her up again before church. Sophie was beginning to like his beat up pick-up with loose change in the cup holders, floor mats filled with dried mud, a backseat filled with seven different ball caps and multiple flannel shirts. Even if Logan weren't in the vehicle, she would still feel close to him by being around his favourite things.

Logan held the door for her as they entered the restaurant. Before Sophie made it to an open booth a woman called her name. Sophie recognized her immediately.

"Irina, hi!" Irina had become a client about one month ago and had since been on three dates with her second match.

The woman waved her over to the booth she sat in with Max, the second match. "I just wanted to thank you again. Date number four right here," she smiled cheekily at Max.

Sophie beamed at the couple. It was always great to see the success of her matchmaking in the flesh. "I'm so glad. You were on this week's list of 'to contact', but now I can see it for myself."

Max spoke up then. "I'll be honest, I was skeptical of the whole matchmaking thing, but I'm so glad my friend convinced me to come to a mixer and sign up. I wouldn't have met Irina otherwise."

"Well then I would ask that you spread the word, Max, I need a few more guys in my database," Sophie joked.

"Already have been. I think I've got a cousin that will be calling shortly."

Irina cut in, "Well, we don't want to hold the two of you up too long. I'm sure you're hungry."

As Logan grabbed her hand to lead her to a table, he added, "You guys have a nice day then." He added a wink as he passed Irina.

They didn't need time to peruse the menu since they were both regulars. As soon as the waitress stopped at their table to pour them each a coffee, Logan and Sophie ordered their meals. While she doctored her coffee with cream and sugar, Sophie thought of something she hadn't before.

What if her and Logan weren't a match?

She swallowed her anxiety and tried to convince herself it was silly. She knew the ins and outs of how the compatibility worked—common interests, shared beliefs, core values, sense of adventure, and now suddenly she couldn't get it out of her mind if Logan and her were well suited.

Her mind wandered with the possible repercussions to her business if she dated someone that wasn't her match while her hand kept a grip on the spoon that continued to stir her coffee.

"Are you alright?"

Logan's quiet question jolted her out of her thoughts. "Uh, yeah. Fine." She didn't meet his gaze from across the table.

"Come on, Sophie."

"It's nothing, really."

"It's something," he argued. "Just tell me. Are you regretting anything about last night?"

"No, of course not," she answered immediately. "I just thought of something, that's all."

"It must have been something important for you to look like someone just stole your puppy. Just spit it out," he encouraged.

"What if we're not a match?" she blurted.

Logan sat there looking at her for only a few seconds before he threw his head back and laughed. Loud.

It wasn't the reaction she expected even though she wasn't quite sure exactly what she assumed his reaction would be. But definitely, not laughing.

"It's not funny."

"Sweetheart, it is," he said between chuckles.

Sweetheart. She liked that. And it took some of the sting away from him laughing at her legitimate concern.

"How?"

"We are," he replied simply.

"Are what?"

"A match," Logan stated while sipping his own coffee.

"How could you know that?"

Logan set his mug down and reached for another creamer. The grin shrunk to a smile and his tone turned serious. "I learned a long time ago that a relationship can only have staying power if both parties work at it. My dad worked at their marriage—or tried, but my mom was working for something else, neglecting what was most important. So. Even looking past everything we already have in common—satisfying jobs, a sense of humour, loving family and friends, our shared love of the Roughriders—"

"Football doesn't really—"

"I'll pretend you never said that," he cut in, "Anyway, like I was saying, even disregarding what we have in common, we both like each other and want to explore that. So we'll work at it—both of us. It makes us a match."

Even though Sophie couldn't quite agree with his philosophy being the matchmaker that she was, Logan's sentiment was sweet and convincing. Almost. She understood the logic that both people in a relationship had to be invested, especially when Logan used the example of his parents, but there were certain factors that determined if that struggle would become a losing battle.

"Could we still make sure?" she asked tentatively.

"Would it make you feel better?"

"Yes."

"Then, sure. But I'd like to eat lunch first."

Their food arrived just as Logan finished his sentence, and they dove in. Sophie rushed through her meal anxious to run their profiles through her software, while she watched Logan leisurely pace himself as he ate. Obviously, he was doing it to tease her. She was certain that she had never seen someone eat quite that slow. Maybe another time when she wasn't feeling uneasy she would've appreciated the amusement of his actions, but now, she just wanted to help him finish his food.

By the time she unlocked the front door to her office a half hour had passed. She practically dragged Logan behind her as they walked from Flatlands.

"It'll take about ten minutes," she said while booting up her computer.

"I've got nothing but time," was his reply accompanied with a cheeky grin.

While the computer ran a search to find Sophie's matches, Logan asked, "So how does it work?" He gestured to her computer.

Sophie was happy he asked. It was fun to talk about the work she loved. "That long questionnaire you filled out? I punch in all your responses, and once that's done, you're saved into the client database. When I run a search for someone it will cross-reference their answers with the answers of the other clients of the opposite sex. It even takes into account that no one wants to date his or her personality twin, so if someone is very similar to you it won't match you at quite a high percentage. The matches that show up for the search will have a match percentage of sixty-five percent or higher."

"Sixty-five? Higher than I thought," he said. And just to egg her on, he added, "What if we're sixty-three?"

She rolled her eyes at him. "I'd let it slide."

"I'd let it slide if it was twenty-three," he stated.

Minutes later the results were listed for Sophie's matches. They were listed from highest percentage to lowest. The first five were not Logan. Then next five weren't either. While Logan peered over her shoulder, she continued to scroll down. He was match number thirteen with a percentage of seventy-one.

"Phew! I barely made it on there," he continued to tease.

Sophie gave a mental sigh of relief and ignored the fact that there were twelve other men within a two hour driving distance that were mathematically better suited for her. She didn't have any interest in them and wouldn't remember their names by tomorrow. She gave Logan a playful punch to the arm.

"This is serious business," she said with a hint of a smirk.

Logan's grin grew thoughtful as his hand on her desk moved to her brush along her jaw. "You're right, it is serious. I know this meant a lot to you, and I'm glad it will give you some peace of mind."

She leaned her head into his palm grateful that he really did understand that this wasn't something she took lightly. Match 'Em Up was her livelihood, and she wouldn't be able to carry on with it if she was living contradictory to it.

"Now," he started, "can we get out of here and enjoy the weather?"

SOPHIE had never had a glass of iced tea quite as satisfying as the one in her hand. Sure it was made from a frozen can of concentrate, but chalk it up to Logan's hand in making it and two slices of lemon to make it extraordinary. It might have also had something to do with her physical location. She was leaned all the way back in a zero-gravity lawn chair on Logan's deck with the sun shining down on her just enough to make her mellow. It was a good place to be.

Logan sat beside her in an identical chair with an identical glass of iced tea. They had come back to his house about an hour ago, and forty-five minutes of that had been spent lying on the deck. They hadn't talked much, but instead listened to the rustle of the leaves, the occasional bellow from the pasture, and just enjoyed the summer sun.

"You know what could make this even better?" Sophie said breaking the silence. She looked over to the chair beside her and found Logan lying back with his ball cap placed over his face. She could only guess that he had nodded off.

But a few seconds later came an "Hmm?"

She smiled and leaned back into her chair. "You with a guitar."

A snort came from under the hat. Then he lifted it from his head. "You serious?" he asked sleepily.

"Yeah."

He grinned at her sincerity. "Be right back."

It took him less than a minute to return with his acoustic. "Any special requests from the audience?" he asked as he slung the strap over his shoulder.

"Your favourites."

This time Logan didn't sing, but simply just lost himself in the melodies. Sophie watched as his body relaxed and gave into the music while his fingers moved over the strings in memorized choreography.

She recognized Johnny Cash's *Happiness is You*, Uncle Kracker's *Smile*, and one of her personal favourites, Emerson Drive's *She's My Kind of Crazy*. During that song, he began to sing just the chorus—all while staring at her with a smile.

She's my kind of Sunday drivin',

Rollin' down the back roads hangin' out the window

Ridin' with her hair in the wind and her hands in the sky, like she's flyin'

She's my kind of ponytail pretty,

Sounds like the country, looks like the city

I march along to whatever outta town drum she plays me,

She's my kind of crazy

He sang the chorus an extra time at the end she assumed to really get the point across that she was now Logan's kind of crazy. They laughed together as he strung out the last word of the song in a long, dramatic note.

Sophie clapped and shouted 'bravo' and 'encore' as Logan stood to take a bow.

A throat cleared from the stairs of the deck. Lincoln stood half way up with his eyes on the guitar in Logan's hands. Sophie looked to Logan and saw that uncertainty now clouded the happiness he had just moments before.

"Uh, I—sorry. I didn't mean to interrupt," Lincoln said tentatively.

"No problem," Sophie answered, "Can I get you some iced tea?"

Still Lincoln's gaze never left the instrument. "No, no. I just wanted to stop by to remind Logan of the meeting tomorrow before peewee signup starts."

Logan spoke up this time, "Thanks, Dad, I remember. But I thought you weren't coaching hockey with me this year."

"I, uh, won't, but Mike wants too. The mayor called my house with a change in meeting time. Starts at six."

"Alright, Dad. Tell Mike we'll catch a ride together."

Sophie observed the exchange with confusion and watched as Lincoln was finally able to meeting Logan's eyes with his own.

There was blatant tension between father and son, and it was obviously caused by Logan holding a guitar.

Lincoln simply nodded before turning around to descend the stairs. But before reaching the final step, he turned back.

"Son," he cleared his throat, "sounded great." And while that statement hung in the air, he left.

Fourteen

There were more people at tonight's Canada Day mixer than Logan expected. The crowd shuffled around the tables, the buffet, and the dance floor unknowing that he sat behind the stage tuning his guitar.

The last few weeks of dating Sophie had been the best two weeks of his life since he was a child. They had so much fun doing regular everyday things together, like just last week when he taught Sophie how to transport bales from the barn to the pasture with the pitchfork on his tractor. It didn't take her long to catch on since she was fairly well versed on driving tractors on her father's farm. Only one bale didn't make the trek out of the five she attempted to move.

They also talked—a lot. About everything. Just a few days ago Logan confided in her about the family problems Mike was going through with his son and his son's mother. He could see Mike was worried about everything—it showed in his work every now and then, and he thought maybe Sophie could keep him in her prayers since he wasn't quite ready for that yet. Sophie was surprised to learn about Caiden, and told him about a few single parents she had as clients. She agreed to keep their family in her prayers.

The following week, Mike seemed to walk around with more pep in his step than before, and Logan wondered if that was because Mike showed up to the first peewee floor hockey practice with his son in tow or if it was a result of Sophie's prayers. He guessed one had to do with the other.

Last week Sophie had tried to convince Mike to attend the upcoming mixer, but he wanted nothing to do with it. Logan found some humour in watching Sophie chase Mike around the shop while desperately explaining how wonderful it could be meeting other single parents, all while Mike banged and crashed any tool he could find to drown her out. She gave up when he finally bellowed, "I already have a woman, I just gotta figure out how to get her back!"

Neither Sophie nor Logan pressured Mike to reveal any more information after that outburst, and they both agreed that Mike would become more social on his own time. When Logan had left home this evening, Mike's truck was parked in its spot near Lincoln's house—Mike had made up his mind about the mixer.

As Logan tuned the last sting on his guitar, he heard Sophie at the microphone. "Good evening, everyone! I'm overwhelmed with tonight's turnout. Maybe I should advertise fireworks at every mixer."

The audience laughed along with her as she continued the evening's welcome and housekeeping rules. Logan tried to concentrate on what she was saying, but his nerves had undeniably sunk in. When she had approached him last week about performing tonight, his first reaction was to laugh off her outrageous idea. He had barely gained the courage to play in front of her, let alone a crowd. But she simply asked him to think about it for a few days. This, of course, had been after the gentlest scolding he'd ever received. He could remember every word.

"Logan, your gift of music is beautiful. Your talent is undeniable. God gives us these abilities to share them—yours just happened to be a gift that's carried in your genes. You should never be ashamed of it. Don't hide your music."

So with that pep talk and the admiration his father's eyes showed that afternoon he'd found him and Sophie on the deck, Logan set out to use his gift.

That night he'd gone through boxes of sheet music and practiced songs he hadn't played in years. He even started a set list if he *were* to play for a crowd. Three days after Sophie had first asked, Logan had convinced himself that he could do it. Although, he still had some reservations. When he officially signed on for the mixer, he ranted to Sophie that he'd never take it past small local crowds and would never pursue anything musically without her knowing. He didn't want to take any chances with the gift that was 'in his genes', as Sophie put it.

After he'd finished spouting off, Sophie had laughed and said, "Are you telling me or yourself?"

Sophie descended the stairs at the back of the small stage and caught Logan's attention as he finished plugging his guitar into the sound system.

"You ready?" she whispered practically giddy.

Logan was pleased with her excitement, although her happiness did nothing to calm the butterflies that had taken up residence in his middle. He could only think of one thing that might help.

"You will pray for me? I'm nervous," he admitted.

Logan didn't miss the quick flicker of shock on her features, but just as quick as it showed it was replaced with a smile. "Absolutely."

She inched close enough to grab his hand. "God, we thank you for today and this opportunity to meet new friends and shine Your light all around us. I want to lift up Logan to You in this minute. Lord, we ask you to calm his nerves and let peace and confidence settle on his shoulders while he shares the beautiful melodies You laid on his heart. Amen."

Almost immediately the butterflies dissipated. But with no time to overthink the little miracle that just occurred inside of him, Logan took the stage.

He stepped up to the microphone while surveying the crowd in front of him. Many faces he recognized, and many he didn't. A lot of those faces had looks of surprise and delight—he wasn't sure if those looks were for him or the prospect of live music, but he ventured on.

He cleared his throat. "It seems a man with do anything for the woman in his life, including overcoming a bad case of stage fright. But I want what she wants, so here goes nothing."

And with only a few strums into his first song, Logan felt at home.

SOPHIE took a moment to observe the crowd as Logan played on stage. The novelty of listening to his musical talent hadn't worn off yet—she loved to listen to him strum and sing. And tonight, others got enjoy what she had all to herself for the last little while.

Some of the people that were at the mixer who were from Sethburn wore expressions of surprise as they recognized their local musician, while others who didn't know Logan looked delighted and enchanted at tonight's live music.

Half way through the first song, the first couple walked onto the makeshift dance floor. It didn't take long for the space she had designated as 'definitely large enough' was packed with people swaying side to side. Most of the couples kept dancing into the next song.

Sophie didn't want to dance with anyone except the man on the stage, so she kept to the side with a glass of fruit punch in her hand. Anna sidled up to her not a minute later.

"Sis, you hid something big from me," she started.

Sophie turned to her sister in confusion. "And what did I hide?"

Anna waved an arm at the stage. "Umm, hello? That Logan is this super awesome, should-have-been-famous rock star. I had no idea."

Sophie giggled. "I didn't either until a couple of weeks ago. Pretty amazing, huh?"

"Yeah."

The night that Logan and Sophie had made things official, she had floated home on a cloud, and when she glided into the apartment she shared with Anna, her sister knew immediately something was up. Sophie told her much of what was happening as of late with Logan and shared that they decided to officially date.

Anna had been shocked given Logan's previous dating tendencies. But when Sophie explained how much he had changed, was asking questions about God, and sharing more private things about himself, which Sophie didn't give details about, Anna had begun to see the light. She was still weary of Logan's spiritual life, as was Sophie, but both women had agreed to keep him in their daily prayers. Anna promised that she would get Drake in on the prayers too.

Last week they had all gone on a double date together. Even though it was a simple outing to the pizzeria, it was the first time Sophie and Logan had spent time with their best friends as a couple. It was also the first time Logan had held her hand all evening as if to declare their new relationship to the public. After the date, Logan had told her that when her and Anna had gone to the washroom at the restaurant, Drake had awkwardly given him the 'intentions' talk. Logan assured him that his goals for the relationship were long term and very serious.

They had both laughed about the conversation, but Sophie was secretly glad that Logan expressed his feelings for her to someone that meant a great deal to them both. She was elated that Drake and Anna were praying for Logan and to have them as a couple to look up to.

Logan transitioned into his third song of the set as Drake came up behind Anna and gave her a kiss on the cheek. Anna blushed at his gesture. They had been a couple almost a year since her sister returned to Sethburn, and Sophie still thought it was adorable how in love they were with each other.

Drake snagged Anna's hand and gave a deep bow in front of her as if he were a knight. "May I have this dance, m'lady?" he exaggerated.

Sophie watched as they skipped to the dance floor and began a simple two-step in time with the upbeat melody. The dance floor became crowded as Logan reached the chorus of the song. There were fewer people sitting at the table than there were dancing—she was definitely going to be busy at work this week. Just by observing, Sophie could already pick out a few potential matches.

Logan's transitioned to the final song of his set. She recognized the cord progression immediately. It was a song he'd been practicing for the past week and had played for her only once to see what she thought. She, of course, had deemed it her favourite. And she solidified her sentiment as he played.

As the dancing couples slowed to keep time with ballad, Sophie began to sway to the music and hummed along. As Logan reached the chorus, his gaze met hers and lingered.

I don't dance, but here I am
Spinning you round and round in circles

It ain't my style but I don't care
I'd do anything with you anywhere
Yes you got me in the palm of your hand 'cause I don't dance

The way Logan sang with such intensity, Sophie knew those lyrics were meant for her. And it made her night. If she wasn't careful, this man would steal her heart without her even knowing it. And she wasn't sure if she'd ever want it back.

LOGAN was coming down from such a high as he drove down the gravel road that led to the ranch. Not only did he finally feel content with enjoying his own musical talent, but he felt thrilled with conquering the stage. Even though the crowd was minimal and filled with people he knew, it still felt like a great big leap in the right direction to contentment. He owed all of the progress to Sophie. Her support in the past few weeks and tonight just moments before he took the stage were necessary in the journey that brought him to now.

He thought again of the short prayer she said with him backstage and the miniature miracle that occurred in him as his nerves calmed to peaceful serenity. It was God, and Logan was ready to admit he owed Him thanks. So for the first time in over a decade, Logan talked to God.

God, thank You for tonight. Thank You for calming my anxiety and allowing me the opportunity to share my talent. Amen.

The verse Mike shared with him some weeks ago came to mind as Logan finished the short prayer. The urgency he felt surrounding those words filled his chest as if to announce it was important that Logan remember those words in that very minute. 'For I know the plans I have for you...plans to prosper you and not to harm you.'

Logan wasn't sure what to do with the sudden intensity, but he recited the words once more in his head before letting the words fade away. He was too excited about this evening's events. When he reached the fork in the drive that led to his house to the left and Lincoln's to the right, Logan made a right turn. He wanted to tell his dad about tonight. He wanted his father to hear that something that used to bring them a lot of sorrow could bring them joy too.

He shoved the gearshift into park and got out of the truck. Before he was able to knock, Mike opened the door only far enough for his shoulder to wedge between the jam as if he was hiding something.

"Logan, it's not a good time," Mike said without meeting his eyes.

His father's voice could be heard, and judging from the volume, Logan guessed he was in the kitchen.

"I just need to talk to Dad. Is he on the phone or something?" he asked trying to peer around Mike.

"No, not on the phone. It's just—"

A feminine laugh drowned out Mike's last words. It was a laugh Logan recognized instantly. It was one he never thought he'd hear again. And one he never wanted to hear again.

His mother had come to Sethburn.

Fifteen

Sophie sat on the bench in front of her garage suite soaking in the Sunday morning sun. Logan was due to pick her up five minutes ago for church. It was unlike him to be late—the other Sundays he was always a few minutes early. She decided to give him just a little longer before she called or sent him a text. Many problems could come up on a ranch any day of the week, so she assumed that the morning chores had put him behind.

She stuck her legs out from under to bench to expose them to the sun. She never tanned much in the summer, but sometimes she'd come away from the season with a light dusting of freckles. While surveying her freckles, Sophie thought of Logan's tan. His was the typical farmer's tan with lines dividing the light and dark skin above his elbows and neck along with his forehead that his ball cap always hid. She teased him about it once which he replied with "guys don't care about their tan" and a shrug.

She checked her watch. Ten minutes late. The service would start in just three minutes, so Sophie dug out her phone and dialed his number. It rang only once before going to voicemail. He probably lost track of time. With no option but to drive herself, Sophie dug for her keys as she walked to her vehicle.

On her way, Sophie felt the urge to pray as she often did when she was driving. It was a good use of quiet time. She thanked God for the gorgeous summer weather, her sister's upcoming nuptials, yesterday's successful mixer, and for Logan. She thanked the Lord for his curiosity about Jesus, his work ethic, his companionship, and she prayed that whatever it was that made him late this morning would work out for the good.

Last night's mixer had been nothing shy of perfect. Several people had come up to her after Logan's set wondering if he would be a regular for open mics around Sethburn. They had been surprised and pleased with his musical talent and wanted to hear more. Logan also had a crowd thank and compliment him after his time on stage. Everyone had a great time, and judging by the couples on the dance floor, she would be busy in the office tomorrow with new and existing clients.

She could hear the congregation sing along to the worship as she climbed the steps to the church doors. She slipped in and spotted a space next to Anna and Drake, then slid into the pew. Anna gave her a questioning look obviously hinting at Logan's absence and Sophie shrugged letting her know that she didn't know where he was either.

The service passed quickly with upbeat songs and a guest speaker who was a missionary that just got back to Canada from building a church in Mexico. The stories and videos had captivated Sophie enough that for an hour she forgot to worry about Logan's whereabouts.

When Pastor Tim ended the closing prayer, Anna was quick to turn to Sophie. "So, where is Logan?"

Sophie dug into her purse and checked her phone. No returned messages. "I don't know. He was supposed to pick me up for church, but after waiting an extra ten minutes, I just drove myself. I still haven't heard from him." Worry crept back in as Sophie's mind wandered to worst-case scenarios.

"Come for lunch with Drake and I. Maybe by then you'll hear from him. It's probably something to do with the cattle," Anna suggested.

Sophie shrugged at her sister's similar assessment. "Okay, let's go."

On the short drive from the church to Flatlands, Sophie's mind had conjured up countless plots and explanations as to why Logan had bailed on her this morning. What if he had grown tired of her and reverted back to playing the field? What if he decided that her faith was really too large of an issue for them to overcome? What if being on stage the night before wasn't something he actually wanted to do but felt forced into it by her instead? What if it was simply a problem with the herd and he was stuck knee deep in a pasture somewhere saving the life of an animal?

There were too many questions swarming around for Sophie to do anything to calm herself down. Their relationship was too new to brush this off as if it was nothing. Logan knew what church and her faith meant to her and to not let her know he would miss it was unlike the Logan she knew for the past month. As she parked, Sophie checked her phone again and still found no word from Logan. She had to remind herself that only the enemy would force that worry into her heart.

She found Drake and Anna in a booth close to the kitchen and plunked down across for them. Carmen was there within seconds to add a third cup of coffee to the table leaving behind a bowl of creamers and sugar packets. Sophie's shoulders slumped as she mixed two creamers into the steaming mug.

"Still nothing," she said with a sigh.

"Maybe something's wrong with your phone. Let me give him a try," Drake said. Five rings and a short voicemail message later, Drake had the same luck as Sophie. "This isn't like him."

Anna nodded in agreement. "If something was up at the ranch, he would've let you know by now. It must be something else."

"Should I try calling Lincoln? I didn't see him in church this morning either," Drake asked.

"Good idea," Anna said.

While Drake pressed his phone to his ear, Sophie decided that she couldn't ask for better friends, and it just so happened those people were her family. She appreciated that they didn't brush off her worry and jumped in to help the situation.

Anna nudged Drake in the side. "You can hang up now." She gestured for the door.

Sophie turned her head to where Anna pointed and spotted Lincoln. And behind him was a gorgeous woman with long brown hair wearing a stylish maxi dress. It was obvious that she was coming in with Lincoln. The woman pushed her sunglasses onto her hair and surveyed the restaurant.

And that's when Sophie recognized her. It was Logan's mother. The glamorous, worldwide country star Stacy-Lynn Freemont was here, and suddenly, Sophie had a very good idea why Logan was nowhere to be found.

Drake hung up the phone and raised his arm to wave at Lincoln. It was obvious that he didn't recognize Stacy-Lynn, and it became clear to Sophie that she and Lincoln were the only two souls in Sethburn who knew about Logan's past.

Lincoln spotted Drake at the booth immediately and began weaving through the tables towards them.

As they reached the table, Lincoln began, "Drake, Anna, Sophie, I'd like to introduce—"

"Stacy-Lynn Freemont," Anna interjected already reaching out her hand to the celebrity.

With a closer look Sophie could see the resemblance between the happy woman in the photograph from almost two decades ago and the one standing in front of her. She had aged beautifully still possessing long, healthy hair, fresh looking skin, and a subtle summer tan. But the smile on her face was what aged her the most—it didn't quite reach her eyes. It wasn't near as sincere as the woman's in the photograph.

Stacy-Lynn grasped Anna's hand awkwardly aware of the potential scene that might erupt if too many more patrons recognized her.

"Nice to meet you," she returned to Anna.

Anna, while unaware of the situation, gave Lincoln a friendly swat. "You didn't tell me you guys knew her. That's a big deal."

Drake shook her hand as well, politely introducing himself.

Before Stacy-Lynn had a chance to shake Sophie's hand, Lincoln cut in, "Stace, this is Sophie—Logan's girlfriend."

What small smile the woman did possess faltered at the mention of her dating Logan, but she quickly recovered, just not quite quick enough to hide some embarrassment.

"So glad to meet you, Sophie. You're very beautiful."

Sophie returned the delicate handshake and simply nodded. She was extremely unsure of how to handle the unfolding scene. Judging by Logan's absence, she assumed his mother's arrival did not go over well, and she wasn't sure which side of the situation to choose. So she decided to remain as neutral as possible for the moment.

"So what brings you to Sethburn?" Anna asked innocently.

"My family," Stacy said.

In that moment, Sophie understood the magnitude of what Logan must be feeling, and she needed to see him. Now. Stacy-Lynn's appearance here must have rocked him to the core.

She slipped from the booth. "I need to be going," she gave Lincoln a squeeze on the shoulder, "You understand."

He nodded and moved to let her by.

LOGAN couldn't keep his thoughts from straying back to last night as he sat at his dining room table peeling the label off of a water bottle.

Stacy had arrived only minutes after Logan had left for the mixer giving her plenty of time to explain whom she was to Mike, who then allowed her entry into Lincoln's house. At least, that's what Mike had tried to explain to him. Logan didn't remember much of what he had been saying since he had been reeling from finding his mother in the house. From what Logan observed in the few minutes he was there, his father seemed practically pleased to see her. And that was what had angered him the most initially.

When Logan had barged in the door past Mike as he continued to insist it was a bad time, Lincoln sputtered at the same time as Stacy began to explain why she was in Sethburn. He had given neither of their excuses the time of day. His reaction had been quick and angry.

First, he had looked at this mother and said, "I was sixteen when I decided I never wanted to see you again—that still stands," and then he looked to his father and asked, "How could you do this—let her come into our home after she destroyed it?"

Then he'd stormed out.

And now he sat in a quiet house, the only sound was the hum of the refrigerator and the soft tumble from the dryer. He ripped off more of the label on the bottle and checked the time. He should've picked up Sophie fifteen minutes ago for church, but he didn't have it in him to face God this morning. Logan gave Him a second shot after connecting with Sophie, but God had proven to ignore him once again. It crushed him to know that she was probably worried about him rather than enjoying Sunday morning with her family in church, but it wasn't as crushing as the knowledge that Stacy-Lynn Freemont, his famous country star of a mother, was just a few hundred feet from him.

A knock sounded at the door, and he glanced up. Make that just a few feet from him. Logan guessed that the sooner he allowed her a few minutes of his time, the sooner she would leave again. He got up to unlock the deadbolt on the front door.

"Mom."

She held up one of two steaming mugs she was holding. "Can I come in?"

Instead of answering, Logan simply stepped back allowing her to pass through into the living room. She offered him the mug on the way by. Coffee was the last thing his mind needed, but he accepted it because it would be ridiculous to argue over coffee when there were larger things that needed to be hashed out.

She stopped between the couch and the coffee table. "You have a beautiful home. Lincoln was telling me last night that the two of you have put a lot of hours into it."

Logan shut the door and still said nothing. She didn't deserve to hear about family projects that she had no part of.

His mother looked almost exactly as she had when she'd left a decade ago. She'd aged well for a fifty-four year old woman. He took a guess that with her wealth, it wouldn't be that difficult to stay looking young. He had kind of hoped that the stress of the fame would have her appearing older than she was, but he wasn't so lucky.

"Do you mind if I sit down?" she asked.

"Yes, but I doubt that'll stop you."

To his surprise, Stacy stayed standing while gripping her coffee cup as if it were a lifeline. Logan found comfort in that he wasn't the only one feeling out of place in this scenario.

"I just wanted to explain a few things."

Logan stared, waiting for her to continue.

Stacy put her mug on the single coaster on the coffee table and clasped her hands together.

"You have a right to angry at me."

Logan snorted.

"I don't expect for you to forgive me right this second, but I want you to know, at least, what happened. Your father and I got married quite young and then he whisked me off to the family ranch. I missed the city, I never adapted to the farm life. Then I had you, and that was a fabulous distraction from my silly woes about not living in the city. But then I went to Nashville, and I just got so caught up in it."

"You're not helping your case," Logan added after what sounded like excuse after excuse.

"I've got to get it all out. I met this agent there—a friend of the friend who I went down there with, and he got me an audition that same afternoon. The label wanted to sign me immediately. It happened so fast. Your father and I had a disagreement about our living situation right before I left. I wanted to move into the city, get a place in the suburbs—move our family, give you more opportunities. Lincoln disagreed. So because I was still angry, I agreed to make a record."

"Don't you dare blame this on a petty argument." Logan's anger grew as she continued.

"I don't blame it on the argument, or Lincoln, or you. I never should have left."

Logan was surprised by her confession. But it was too late to make it right. Coming back after a decade didn't make it right. "But you did."

Stacy remained quiet—guilt painted her face and her body language said the same.

"And you're famous now. You got what you wanted, Mom."

"I didn't."

"Too bad it took ten years for you to realize that."

A single tear trailed down her cheek, but Logan didn't feel any remorse for any of the things he said.

"I'm so sorry, Logan. I'd do anything just to have you back."

Logan couldn't handle the conversation a second longer. He stalked to the front door and held it open. Stacy took the hint and walked through it and away from him all while swiping at her cheeks, coffee mugs forgotten.

He slammed the door with force and paced the living room not daring to look out the window in fear of seeing her still standing outside. He needed to throw something, yell, fight.

He stormed into the only room that held memories of her and grabbed the one thing that could only make it better. Then he took it outside, raised it high above his head, and slammed it down against the deck railing.

Strings and wood and metal fell to the ground in shattered pieces. Just like his heart.

SOPHIE made it from Flatlands to Logan's ranch in record time. She guessed the damage had already been done, but maybe there was a chance she could piece it back together.

She got out and raced up the front steps. Her fist hurt with her forceful knocks.

"Logan, you here?" she called.

Silence answered her, so she headed around the back towards the deck. And what she found confirmed her fears.

Logan's guitar was completely destroyed.

Sixteen

Logan's cellphone vibrated along the counter top as he poured milk into his bowl of Cheerios. It was the sixth text message he'd received already this morning—second message from Sophie. One was from Mike about their work plans for the day, and the other two were from his dad, which was weird since his father had never sent him a single text message in the eight years he'd had a cellphone up until yesterday. Logan blamed his mother for teaching Lincoln—it was the only reasonable explanation. Phone calls had worked just fine before. Although, he would've ignored that too.

The only message he would reply to would be Mike's, which he did while eating breakfast. He shoved his phone into his back pocket while turning the dishwasher on, although he wasn't sure why he needed it. It wasn't like he would be answering any calls today anyway. He wasn't in the mood to listen to apologies that were too late or advice that he didn't want to hear.

Today would be a busy day on the ranch, and Logan hoped that it would be enough to keep his mind off of his mother's arrival. He also hoped he could put Sophie to the back of his mind because he didn't want to think about what she might be going through right now with him ignoring her messages and giving her no idea about his goings on.

With Stacy-Lynn in Sethburn, around his father and his ranch, Logan was confused and angry with a lot of things. Including his relationship with Sophie. There had been a reason why he didn't have long-term relationships with the women he dated. It put him at risk of being hurt just like what happened with his mother. And now that he'd taken a chance on Sophie, Logan was wondering if it had been the right choice.

All of his earlier fears came flooding back. What if years from now, Sophie left him for greener pastures? What if they got married and started a family and then she decided the life they shared wasn't good enough? He had lived through that nightmare once—he didn't want to do it again.

Logan found Mike checking over the horse trailer they used for transporting cattle. This week Mike was taking a load of the spring calves to the auction in Saskatoon, and they only had today to prepare everything. It was just what he needed to ignore his scattered thoughts.

The two men worked in silence doing an inspection on the horse trailer, fixing the brakes, and sweeping it out. They worked together herding the calves going to the auction into the holding pen where they would spend the night before loading them onto the trailer early the next morning. Logan even spent a few extra minutes calming Eighty-four down as she too wanted to join her friends in the holding pen even though she wasn't going to the auction.

It was lunchtime before Logan and Mike took their first break. Mike invited him back to the main house where Stacy-Lynn had promised fresh tuna sandwiches, but Logan hastily declined that invitation while wiping the sweat from his brow.

"You can't avoid them forever, man," Mike replied quickly after Logan declined the sandwiches.

Logan knew Mike spoke the truth, but he wasn't ready yet. It was still too soon. "You're right, but I need a little more time. I've got leftover lasagna Sophie made last week I'm willing to split if you'll join me at me place."

Mike shrugged. "Sounds good to me."

They walked to Logan's house without conversation, and Logan was grateful that his friend understood Logan's predicament about taking him up on his offer for lunch. It was too motherly for Stacy to be making him a meal just like she once did. He wasn't ready for playing nice and acting like everything was all right.

Logan dished up two hearty servings, stuck them in the microwave, and hit 'Popcorn' not bothering with punching in an exact time. He produced two cans of Coca-Cola from the fridge and tossed one to Mike over the kitchen island.

Mike finished his plate first and pushed it aside while reaching for the last of his pop. "So, you going to tell me what all the family drama's about?"

"Do I have to?" Logan asked while shoving the last bite into his mouth.

"Well, I'm living with your dad who you haven't spoken to since Saturday. And this woman who looks strangely like you shows up on the weekend. Her and Linc spent the last two evenings in deep conversations upstairs at the kitchen table, which makes it awkward when all I want is five minutes to make a grilled cheese sandwich but instead, I had to head to Flatlands because breaking up those conversations seemed like the most awkward situation ever. So yeah, it'd be nice to know what's going on."

Logan snorted at Mike's attempt at comic relief. "Like you haven't guessed who she is."

"You mean have I guessed that she's one of the most famous country stars on the continent *or* that she's your mother?"

Logan grunted in reply.

"Look, man, I've only known you a little while, and from what I gathered, you are not close with that woman. In fact, I never asked about her because neither you nor your dad have any family pictures that exist before you graduated. I took that as a sign to not bring it up. But what I do know is that you and Linc are tight. Don't lose that."

Logan went into defensive mode as Mike's word hit too close to home. "You've got no idea what really happened. What kind of woman decides that fame is more important that her family? Her—she's that woman. There isn't any coming back from that sense of abandonment that she left us with. Here one day, gone the next. And now he takes her side? Just like that! Come on." He was breathing hard after his rant. Anger boiled to the surface as he gave more information than he should have.

"You haven't heard him out. I don't think that's how it went down," Mike answered calmly, clearly unfazed by Logan's tirade.

"Sure looked like it to me judging from the messages I got from Dad."

"Hear him out. Remember this—if the mother of my child came back into my life, I would be absolutely foolish to ignore the fact that we had a chance to be a family again. Not instantly, but maybe in the future. Relationships between a parent and his son are irreplaceable. I would know."

The sound of Mike's chair sliding back against the hardwood was all that could be heard in the quiet house as he left Logan to think about what was just said.

IT was Monday evening, and Sophie had yet to hear from Logan. She was beyond concerned and couldn't think about anything else. She had left multiple voicemails—which she was sure the last one sounded seriously desperate—and sent several text messages. Now she was brainstorming another way to contact him. Even if she just got confirmation that he was okay, that would be enough.

She brought up the Yellow Pages app on her phone and search for Lincoln Fraser's home phone number. It began ringing in seconds.

"Hello?"

A female voice was not what Sophie had expected. She guessed it was Logan's mother.

"Hi, this is Sophie. Is this Stacy-Lynn?"

"Yes, dear. I met you at the restaurant yesterday, right?"

"You did. I was, uh, wondering if you knew where Logan was?" she asked trying to mask her worry.

"Let me peek across the yard. Hold on." Sophie heard rustling and footsteps. "His truck is home, which would mean he's within a few hundred acres of here."

"Okay, thanks." Sophie felt weird talking with the stranger. She hadn't heard good things about her and yet she seemed very polite at Flatlands yesterday. It wasn't sitting right, and she wanted to get off the phone as quickly as possible.

"Umm, Sophie?" Stacy asked, as she was ready to hang up.

"Yes?"

"I don't know how much you know about our family, but given what Lincoln has told me about your relationship with Logan, I thought maybe I could explain a few things."

Sophie felt even more awkward now. It was as if she was going behind Logan's back to get information. "Not to be rude, but I know quite a bit about Logan's childhood and I won't be choosing any sides if that's what you were hoping to accomplish."

"No, not at all," Stacy answered immediately. "I just wanted you to know what happened, so that you can understand what Logan might be going through."

"That's fine. I know the basic events that led up to your departure when he was a teenager."

"Can I tell you what happened since then?"

Again, Sophie became uneasy. "I think it's best if Logan shares it with me."

"Honey, from what I've heard, you're a part of this family now. So I'd like you to hear it from me. Maybe it would do you some good to hear both sides."

Sophie wasn't sure what to do with her conflicting emotions after Stacy-Lynn divulged her new status in the Fraser family. She was flattered Lincoln had considered her enough a part of the family to tell Stacy-Lynn; however, she hadn't decided if this was information she really needed to have.

But the woman didn't give her time to decide. "I'm sure that if you weren't aware before you met me yesterday, you are now privy to the information that I have had a fairly reasonable career in music. I worked my way up the ladder quite quickly after I left for Nashville. I was playing stadiums a year after my first album came out. I had a manager, an agent, a stylist, you name it. They became a substitute family of sorts for the better part of a decade. But still, every single night when I'd try to fall asleep, my mind would wander back to what I left on our ranch. Do you know anything about soul mates, Sophie?"

"A little."

"Well, hun, then you would know that when a person finds a soul mate, that's the only person that can ever make you happy. So every night I would think about Lincoln, and I would drift off to sleep with peaceful dreams. But I never went back."

"If he was your soul mate, why didn't you?"

"I thought it was too late. I had severed the relationship with Lincoln and destroyed the one with my son. Who would be willing to take me back after I did something so horrible?"

Stacy-Lynn was right about her guess—Logan didn't want her back. But she didn't share Logan's opinion with her. Instead, she asked, "So why come back now?"

"Eventually, I couldn't sleep anymore. The guilt was too much. My need to be near Lincoln was too overwhelming. The fame and success had done nothing to help me forget about what I left behind. My stylist goes to church when we're not on the road, and she brought me along about a month ago. I'll never forget the passage of Scripture the pastor preached about that Sunday. Ephesians 4:31-32."

Sophie knew the verse. It was one she had found shortly after Logan told her about his childhood, but she hadn't had the courage to share it with him yet. She started reciting it, "I know it well. 'Get rid of all bitterness, rage and anger, brawling and slander, along with every form of malice. Be kind and compassionate to one another, forgive each other, just as Christ forgave you.'"

Sophie heard a sniff from the other line and guessed Stacy-Lynn had begun to cry. "It's a beautiful verse, isn't it?" The other woman said. "Once I heard that passage I knew I had to take a chance. I had to know if Lincoln could look past what I'd done, forget his anger and forgive me so I could have my family back in my life. That day, I decided to live my life according to that verse.

Because if I couldn't get rid of all the negative emotions in my life, why would Lincoln or Logan do that for me?"

"And are you glad you came back?"

"I am. Lincoln and I have talked. It won't be easy, but we want to work on getting back what we had before I messed it all up. I'm going to live in Sethburn indefinitely, so we can both fully commit to the process."

If nothing else, Sophie was glad that Lincoln was looking for happiness again. The uncertainty of Logan's attitude and unwillingness to forgive was an entirely different story. She knew that if Lincoln welcomed Stacy-Lynn back into his life, their father-son relationship would be tested.

"Logan will be harder to win over," she said.

Stacy-Lynn let out a huff. "Don't I know it. Are you a praying woman, hun?"

"I am."

"Then pray for the both of us. I know you won't choose sides—that's good, but pick God's side. Pray His will be done."

"I can do that," she promised, since she was already doing that.

"And, hun?"

"Yes?"

"He just walked into his house. He's home."

BARELY twenty minutes had gone by from the time Sophie hung up the phone with Stacy-Lynn to the time she was driving up Logan's driveway. She tried to come up with what she wanted to say to Logan on the drive over, but couldn't seem to get the words right. She hoped that their relationship could continue on just as it was and that Logan's new interest in God would be enough to carry him through facing his past.

Before getting out of her car, she prayed. *God, guide us through this conversation. Give me the right words, and open Logan's heart to what You want him to hear. Amen.*

She made it up the front steps to the door without seeing or hearing any signs from inside. But she knocked anyway not knowing if Logan would even answer the door.

Almost a minute went by before Sophie heard the deadbolt turn. Logan opened the door only as wide as his shoulders. He looked bone-tired, ready to drop, weary to the core, and unhappy to see her at the door. His eyes stayed at her feet, and he said nothing.

She cleared her throat. "Can I come in?"

Logan turned around and headed into the house, leaving the door open behind him. She took that as an invitation and slipped inside. She found Logan sitting on the couch facing the living room window, so she sat across from him on the loveseat.

"I met your mother yesterday."

His eyes snapped to hers, but still he said nothing.

"She and your dad came into Flatlands while I was having lunch with Drake and Anna after church." She paused wondering if he'd say anything about him standing her up yesterday, but he remained quiet.

"Anyway, I hadn't heard from you since Saturday, and then when I met Stacy I understood why. I mean, it's a lot to take in—everything you went through, then suddenly she just shows up here out of the blue. Since you weren't answering my texts or calls, I just wanted to make sure you were all right. I called your dad's house a little while ago. She answered. We had a good talk."

"What are you, best friends now?" he sneered.

Sophie took a deep breath instead of reacting to Logan's angry remark. She needed patience to get through this. It was obvious he was upset and ready to direct it at whoever was in his path, but he needed to hear what she had to say.

"Logan, I'm not choosing sides. This is your family. But I do want to explain a few things about myself in light of what your mom told me. Will you let me?"

Logan nodded reluctantly.

"You're mom told me why she's here now. She told me that your dad and her are soul mates—no fame or success or money ever replaced what she felt for Lincoln and you. She made a mistake leaving, a big one, but she's here to stay and work on things with you and your dad. She wants your family back."

Logan's eyes were filled with moisture, tears waited to make their escape down his face. "It's too late, Sophie. She can't come back from what she did to me, to us."

Sophie's heart was breaking listening to the hurt in his voice, but she carried on. "What you don't understand Logan is that you have the power to make this happen. So does your father. With God's help, and with a lot of forgiveness, nothing but good things can come from this situation."

"You don't know that. You don't know what it's like," he snapped.

"You're right, I have no idea. But let me tell you this—I started my business because I believe in finding your soul mate. God created people for us to share our earthly lives with, and I want everyone to find that. *I* want to find that. Your parents found that. And yes, it will take some time for them to get back to what they were, but they have God on their side.

God wants us to live our lives to the fullest, and that includes relationships of all kinds. Just look how he's already blessed you and I with that. Drake has been your best friend for years; you guys are two peas in a pod. Your relationship with your father rivals the best father-son bond anywhere. I found my best friend in my very own sister. We are blessed. And we can add even more to that if we trust God."

"It's not that easy."

"I never said it would be, but it's worth the chance."

They sat quietly for a few moments, and Sophie hoped some of what she said would sink in for Logan. His hurt had built a wall around his heart and only God had the tools to break those barriers.

"I want to share this verse with you, and then I'll go," she said. Sophie recited the same verse she spoke about with Stacy-Lynn and prayed that the man she cared so deeply for would have the ability to rid himself of his anger and grab hold of God's compassion and the power of forgiveness.

Seventeen

The verse Sophie recited to him was like a punch to the gut. *Get rid of all forms of malice. Be kind and compassionate, forgiving one another.* Logan struggled to fight against the heavy weight of guilt that was pressing down on his shoulders.

He had to resist those feelings—his mother had been gone so long, he couldn't forgive that easily. He couldn't dig deep enough inside himself to find that sort of compassion to look past the lonely decade she was missing from their family. Logan needed her to see first hand the hurt she caused to her only child. He wanted her to just have a glimpse of what it was like.

Logan sat on the couch waiting for Sophie to say more after she read the verse. But she said nothing. Instead, she stood from the loveseat and joined him on the couch. Logan didn't dare look at her because he knew that her charming eyes and kind words would draw him into the place she wanted him to be. A place he wasn't ready for.

Her arm slid across his shoulders, and her lips touched his cheek.

"I'll be praying for you," she said.

The front door clicked shut just seconds later, and he was alone with his thoughts once again. Except his feelings stayed with the woman who just left. Since his mother's arrival, Logan hadn't given much thought to his relationship with Sophie. And if he did, he was sure that she would convince him to handle the situation her way—brushing over it with kindness and grace.

So for now he'd ignore his feelings for her as much as he could. He would try to forget the memories he'd made with her over the summer. He would dismiss the night they first danced together at one of Match 'Em Up's mixers, the way she felt encircled in his arms as if he would protect her from anything bad that would ever happen. He would overlook the time he picnicked with her in the park watching her beautiful hair blow in the breeze and her even more gorgeous smile light up when he said something she thought was funny. He would turn a blind eye to the way he felt right before, during, and immediately after he kissed her for the first time—the feeling of rightness that settled around him when she was so close to him. He would forget about the moment when he played her the song they danced to—sharing his hidden talent for the first time. And he would pay no attention to the hope that overwhelmed him whenever he thought about saying three very important words to her that would change both of their lives forever.

He was going to put all of that out of his mind.

SOPHIE watched Logan's house grow smaller in the rear view mirror of her car until the dust made it disappear. That hadn't gone how she'd hoped.

Why wouldn't God have given her the right words to break through Logan's hurt? She thought that verse would have been just what he needed to hear. But instead of still sitting in his living room leaning against him while watching the sunset knowing that everything will work out just fine, she was on her way home, expanding the distance between them.

Maybe this was her wake up call. This could be the warning she needed to slow down her involvement with Logan. This could be the sign that she wasn't cut out for the job of bringing Logan back to Jesus—it was time for reinforcements like a pastor or Logan's father.

But as hard as she tried to picture her life, her future, without Logan in it as a permanent fixture, she couldn't. He was there in her hopes and dreams, in every part of it—her heart had decided that weeks ago without her permission.

So she did what she always resorted to in a fearful situation, Sophie prayed.

LOGAN swung the duffle bag over his shoulder as he shut the back door. Mike would be almost finished loading the calves into the trailer, so he didn't have much time to catch him before he left.

Last night, Logan had slept in fits only getting just over two hours of sleep of the six he spent lying in bed. He kept dreaming of Sophie. He would fall back into the same dream after every time he woke up. She was sitting in a pew inside the church smiling at him. Her face was angelic, her hair glowing, her eyes sincere. The image was so peaceful and serene; it was as if Sophie would stay in that state as long as it took for him to catch up to her. Logan had finally pulled himself out of bed after the third dream at four-thirty. It was then he decided he needed to get away.

After a brisk walk down to the shop, he found Mike latching the back door of the trailer with the calves ready to go.

"Mike, hey, I'm going to take 'em," he shouted over the racket the calves were making.

Mike looked up to focus on Logan. "Take who where?"

Logan gestured to the trailer. "I'll go the auction. You can stay back. I need to get out of here." He hoped Mike didn't ask too many questions. Logan just wanted to get on the road as fast as he could, get as far away from his mother, his problems, all of his thoughts, everything.

Confusion took over Mike's features. "Uh, okay, boss."

"Everything ready to ride?" Logan asked as he slung his bag into the back seat of the truck.

"Just one last brake light check. I haven't finished the registration forms yet, that'll have to be done once you get there."

Logan nodded already on his way to the driver's side door. "I'll take care of it. Call me if you need anything."

Mike rushed to the door as Logan hopped in and started the vehicle. "Hey man, I know why you're rushin' off, but it's not going to solve anything."

Logan sighed as he stared out the windshield. "I've told you this before, but you don't understand."

"That's what you think. I'll be prayin' for you." With that Mike gave a hearty two taps to the hood and walked off leaving Logan free and clear to drive away.

So he did.

Logan checked his cell phone once he had pulled the trailer safely into the parking lot where the sale would take place. He found nine text messages and five missed calls. It made him glad he had turned his phone to silent for the two-hour drive.

Ignoring the messages from his dad, Logan opened the only one he had received from Drake.

I had to hear from Mike that you left town five days before my wedding. Call me.

Logan winced. He'd forgotten about his best friend's wedding with all the drama on the weekend. He hadn't been there for

Drake lately with his relationship with Sophie taking priority and now with his mother in town. He owed his best friend some quality time, yet he wasn't even in town the week before his wedding. Some best man he was. But still, Logan couldn't bring himself to regret his impromptu trip—he needed some time away from everything.

The auction would start tomorrow and was only two days. He'd be home on Thursday with plenty of time to help out until Saturday. He sent him a quick reply.

I'll be back Thursday a.m. and free to help until Saturday. Sorry, man.

Surely Drake would understand his situation if he knew the details. Logan would explain everything when he got back. He opened the first of three messages from Sophie.

Thinking of you today. xo

Logan wished she wasn't but didn't have it in him to be sad that he was in her thoughts. He skipped to the next one.

Lincoln let me know you'll be gone a few days. I hope it helps. Drive safe xo

And finally. *Miss you already. Let me know when you're safe.*

Logan didn't send a reply. It was time to focus on the job at hand. And he had no idea what to say to her anyway.

An hour and a half passed by the time Logan made it to the front of the line and filled out the necessary paperwork to register his cattle. The registration table was stuffed into a small office at the arena that was overcrowded and awfully smelly, putting Logan in an even fouler mood. It took another two and a half hours to unload the livestock, ensuring his were all tagged correctly, then navigating his truck and trailer out of the overflowing lot.

It was late afternoon by the time Logan checked into his hotel. And with nothing to do until later that evening when the host company of the auction would hold a large barbeque at the arena, he found himself surfing the channels without settling on anything interesting. Not even the Toronto Blue Jays could keep his attention. The last few restless nights were catching up to him, and Logan decided to doze.

The clock read ten p.m. when he woke up from the loud growl of his stomach. He had skipped lunch while getting everything settled at the arena, and now he had slept through the entire barbeque. Without even rolling over, Logan reached for the hotel phone and ordered some room service.

A half hour later with a late night burger filling him up, Logan fell right back to sleep dreaming of one very beautiful woman that was too stubborn to escape his thoughts.

Logan woke early and made it the arena with a steaming cup of Tim Horton's coffee in his hand a full hour before the auction would begin. He recognized several fellow ranchers from around the area as he made his way through the crowds, ones from as far north as Beauval, which was three hours farther than Sethburn.

He greeted several farmers and chatted with them about live-stock prices, ranching, and the like. He loved the atmosphere—it did wonders to take his mind off all his other problems. As time grew closer to the start of the auction, Logan's mood shifted into something much lighter than it had been in days.

The fluorescent lights had gone from dim to bright above the shoots in the middle of the arena. The bleachers surrounding them began to fill with ranchers, farmers, and their families. The line at the concession grew larger as more people filed inside and needed their morning coffee jolt. The familiar sent of cattle and hay clung to the air in the large room making him feel right at home. The volume and excitement levels rose as the auctioneer took the stage. Logan settled in his seat ready to watch people bid higher and higher for each group of cattle.

His cattle made it through the shoot just before the auction would break for lunch, and the group was sold for one of the highest prices per pound so far. Knowing he'd be going home with a big cheque, Logan splurged on lunch getting the rack of ribs with potato salad and corn on the cob. He found a seat at a table with several other men he recognized.

"Afternoon," he nodded to them all as he set his tray down.

The men all tipped their hats and the women at the table gave him wave, some of them greeting him by name. Most of the ladies were wives of the men at the table spending the day with their husbands enjoying the auction. It reminded Logan that just a few weeks ago he had promised Sophie he'd bring her to one of these events. She would have loved it—the sites, the sounds, the smells, the energy and excitement of the crowd. She would have got a kick out of watching the crowds as the children hopped from one bleacher to the next searching for pop cans or bottles that were discarded in order to take them to the canteen for a five cent candy, or as the wives separated from their husbands and families to congregate together for some girl time. Logan could picture her handing out flyers to the single men and women for her next mixer, charming them with her kind eyes and sweet smile. And no doubt, they would all come to the event just to catch another glance of their matchmaker.

But half way through his rack of ribs, Logan's thoughts came to a screeching halt. Sophie wasn't here to enjoy today. And he didn't know if she ever would be because after the nightmare of the last weekend, Logan didn't know if he was willing to risk his heart for another woman he loved. The reminders of the hurt he lived knowing his mother left for something greater and the loneliness he felt growing up without her were too fresh and too jagged to envision any type of future with a woman in it.

But one thing was for sure—after deciding that love wasn't worth the chance, Logan had never felt as lonely as he did right then.

Eighteen

The second day of the auction started out with much less excitement than the day before. The concession line up was half the size as the previous morning, the announcer was looking a little worse for wear, and the stands were much scarcer. Today, only bulls were up for sale, and Logan wasn't interested. But he was still using the arena as a hide out. After yesterday afternoon's realization, Logan wallowed in his sorrows, isolating himself from facing all that was his past, and away from the people that reminded him of it.

He didn't taste much of his double-double this morning, but appreciated the caffeine jolt it provided. Last night he hadn't gotten more than a couple hours of rest. He found a spot along the sideboards adjacent to the shoots in the center and leaned heavy against them. This morning, he simply didn't have the energy to stand up right, and the stairs to the bleachers looked daunting. He pulled his hat low on his forehead and focused on the shoots in front of him hoping that all the ranchers would pass him by. It was no surprise he wasn't up for conversation. The first hour passed slowly but gained momentum when a rather rowdy bull took the stage. He knocked over a few shoots; scaring the auctioneer enough that he threw his microphone at the animal in self-defense.

As the first group of bulls was ushered from the arena, the announcer stated there would be a fifteen-minute break. Then Logan felt someone shoulder up beside him. He should be thankful that the people had held off this long since normally he treated these auctions as the social event of the year. Logan didn't bother looking over. The man would start a conversation soon enough— or maybe he would just leave. Several minutes passed and the man hadn't budged. Finally Logan snuck a look.

Drake stood shoulder to shoulder with him in a similar pose—one knee cocked and both elbows resting on the ledge of the sideboards.

"Hey," Drake said, as if it was expected that he was at the auction two hours away from Sethburn just days before his wedding.

Logan did his best to hide the shock on his face. It was a quite a drive for him to make from Sethburn instead of simply calling him. But what was more alarming was that the initial reaction to seeing his best friend was almost happiness. Was the loneliness getting to him already?

"What are you doing here?" Logan asked looking away in an attempt to hide his emotions.

"Had to see if I've still got a best man in, oh—" Drake checked his watch dramatically, "seventy-two hours, give or take."

Logan huffed. "I told you that you did when I texted you yesterday," he explained.

"Vaguely. It's one of those things a guy's got to be sure about."

"Well, you do," Logan insisted.

"Good to know. I best tell Anna there's no need for rein-forcements." Drake took out his phone and sent off a quick text message.

Logan sighed knowing that he had slacked off at a time when Drake was really counting on him. "I'm sorry, man. I won't let you down, I promise. There's just a lot going on right now."

Drake chuckled. "No kidding. Met your mother on Sunday. And since my best friend failed to tell me she was a country super-star and that the reason he moved to my town ten years ago with only just his father was because of her, I had to figure all that out by myself. And once I had done that, I figured out why you were missing in action. Simple physics really."

Logan rubbed his hands over his face feeling foolish that Drake had to hear about his childhood from someone other than himself. When it was summed up like that by a friend who was able to make light of Logan's giant mistake, Logan wished he had told him sooner.

"Yeah, okay. I should have told you," Logan admitted.

Drake grabbed onto Logan's shoulder. "Hey, it's a hard thing to explain, I get it. But it wouldn't have mattered to me. Actually, now that I know, it explains a lot more about you than I knew before."

"It does, huh? How's that?"

"I understand a little bit more about your dating life. I'm guess-ing the serial dating had something to do with your mom. Your faith too—I'm glad that's changing though," Drake regarded him skeptically before asking, "Right?"

Logan shifted his gaze. He had been avoiding thoughts about God since Saturday. He was angry—how could He let this happen? God took away his mother, and then when He sends her back, Logan was just supposed to forgive? *Yeah, right.*

"It was," Logan stated quietly, "but not so much right now."

Drake gave Logan another comforting pat on the back. "I understand it can be tough, but don't give up. How are things with you and Sophie through all this then?"

Logan was surprised Drake hadn't heard about their relationship woes through Anna by now, but he was grateful that Sophie hadn't disclosed everything he was struggling with. But the question still weighed heavy on his mind because it reminded him that he was going to have to let her go—his heart couldn't risk loving again. "Not good. I'm, uh—her and I need to talk when we get home. I don't think it's going to work out."

Drake leaned back against the boards again moving his gaze to the shoots in front of them. He stayed quiet for a few moments, and Logan felt a weary anticipation as to what he would say next. But what Drake said did nothing short of rocking him to the core.

"You know that feeling you get when you share a meal with Sophie, that simple feeling of contentment, like you're just happy to being sitting beside her and need nothing more than that? Do you remember how it felt to have your arm around her while enjoying a quiet evening at home, as if nothing could ever top that moment, not even something as big as winning a lottery? How did you feel when you shared your music with Sophie for the first time—I bet it was completely exhilarating finally sharing that with the person you cared so deeply for. And what about all the things you haven't experienced with her yet—waking up with her every morning, daily chores, lazy Saturday mornings, maybe have children one day, grow old with her. What about all of that?"

Logan's heart thudded in a heavy, fast rhythm as his thought about all those things, those experiences, with Sophie. It had crossed his mind, sure, when weighing the odds about if their relationship would carry on, but he hadn't sunk his teeth into the matter, so to speak. Until now.

Drake continued, "Logan, that's what you're giving up. When Anna left for Toronto last summer while I was still in the hospital, she hadn't contemplated any of that. She decided she couldn't handle the current situation because of things that had happened years before. She needed to escape so fast that she didn't think about the way it would affect the future—not just hers. I was devastated when I found out she left. Her decisions affected me too. So let me ask you this—what will Sophie's future look like?"

Logan's mind was reeling with questions. Could he really imagine his future without her in it? Without her, wouldn't it be complete misery? And how would this choice he was willing to make affect her future? Would she move on without him, and could he even handle watching her live her life without him in it?

"Let me leave you with one more thing. Romans 13 says 'Love does no harm to a neighbour'," Drake paused, then added, "Now you've got to figure out if you really love her." And with one final heavy pat to Logan's shoulder, Drake said, "See you tomorrow."

LOUD music wafted through the windows of Logan's house so everyone in the backyard could hear it. Picnic tables were set up near the deck for extra seating and a circle of lawn chairs surrounded the fire pit to accommodate the twenty or so guests attending. Food was spread all over the place, with hot dogs and roasting sticks near the fire, a roaster of warm burgers sat near the barbeque, bags of chips were on every table, and ice cream was being scooped into waffle cones and passed around.

Several lawn games were set up around the house, including horseshoes, bocce ball, and ladder golf. People were beginning to settle into the chairs around the fire to ward off the evening chill, while others continued the 'Lawn Game Olympics' as Drake so astutely name them. With less than two days of planning, Logan could say that Drake and Anna's joint bachelor and bachelorette party was a success.

After what Drake said at the arena Tuesday afternoon, Logan decided to come home that night instead of staying until Wednesday. It was time for him to step up his best man duties—the wedding was only a few days away after all. When he pulled into the ranch Tuesday night, his mother was outside to greet him and invited him over for supper. Logan had been physically and emotionally exhausted and didn't feel like cooking a meal, so he had agreed despite his emotions.

The conversation had been stilted, but Mike and Lincoln did their best to keep the meal as peaceful as possible. Logan shared that he would be busy planning for the next few days, so Lincoln would have to pitch in with the ranch chores as much as possible. As soon as he said the word 'party', his mother had offered her services. Logan wasn't sure if it was simply a bribe to get his forgiveness in turn or if her offer had been genuine. But since he didn't have a lot of party planning skills and he was ready to ask Sophie for her input, he agreed to let his mother help. He assigned Stacy-Lynn with planning the food, and he managed to put the rest together himself. And judging by a quick glance around the yard, it looked like he'd pulled it off.

When Sophie first arrived, their greeting had been awkward. Logan had avoided her since he came back on Tuesday, and it probably wasn't the best idea to have waited until tonight to finally see her. His first impression as she stepped out of Anna's car was that she looked absolutely breathtaking. It seemed as if every time he saw her Sophie's beauty was a new kind of surprising. And tonight, he wasn't disappointed. Her hair fell to her shoulders in soft waves, she wore little make-up—his favourite look of hers, and a modest summer dress just casual enough for the occasion.

It reminded him of the many times he told her she was beautiful. Sometimes it was during a meal when they were telling each other about their day, other times it was when she dressed up for their date, and occasionally, he told her that when she was leaning on his shoulder watching a Riders game with him. It didn't matter what hairstyle or outfit she chose or how much make-up she wore, Sophie always looked gorgeous.

Only when she climbed the steps to his door, did Logan remember that maybe he shouldn't be doing that anymore—telling her how beautiful she was inside and out, even though he'd never stop thinking it. With the intentions he had to break it off with Sophie after the weekend was over, it was no longer his place to be the man telling her that. And it ripped him apart as she entered his home, and he didn't say those words.

For two days now, Logan had been replaying Drake's words in his mind. *Love does no harm to a neighbour.* And he kept debating whether or not leaving Sophie would be harming her or helping her. She didn't deserve a man who could never learn to trust her completely, but on the other hand, Logan couldn't imagine his future without Sophie by his side.

Logan settled into a cushy lawn chair next to Drake pitching into the conversation when prompted, while repeatedly catching glances of the woman he longed to spend the evening with. He was glad to see her enjoying time with Anna and her other friends, but he would rather be the one putting that smile on her face.

If only it were that simple.

SOPHIE tossed her last horseshoe at the target missing it by mere inches. She and Jill, one of Anna's friends, had been playing for almost an hour, half of that was trying to break the tie. So far, the evening had only a few awkward moments, but luckily, they were ones that were over with quickly so that Sophie could enjoy the evening celebrating with Anna and Drake.

Earlier on the ride to Logan's ranch, Anna spent more time helping Sophie prepare herself emotionally for tonight than they did conjuring excitement for the event. And for that, Sophie felt terrible. Once the initial meet and greet was over, she had set a goal to make sure her mind was focused on the reason for tonight—the bachelor and bachelorette party. However, Sophie would admit that her gaze had wandered a few times already.

Sunday—five days ago—was the last time Sophie had spoken to Logan. It was when she had left him with the verse from Ephesians to think about. When Anna met her at home on Monday telling her that Drake found out Logan left Sethburn for a few days, Sophie had become anxious and worried for his state of mind. But even though she sent a few text messages to him, she received no reply. So when Logan greeted her at his front door tonight she had no idea what to say to him.

In the last few days after hearing nothing from Logan, Sophie couldn't ignore that their relationship was disintegrating. Rapidly. Since he obviously had no intentions of communicating with her, she did the only thing she could think to do—she prayed. But God hadn't provided any answers for Sophie. Yet instead, a sense of calm had washed over her about the situation. Her anxiety had shrunk to a minimum, and she was able to get a few good nights of sleep in the midst of a hectic week. And now even though she had no certainty of the outcome or a look into her future, Sophie continued to pray.

Every now and then she had a moment of sadness, maybe even a bit of premature mourning of what they had, like the minute she saw Logan waiting at the front door for her like he had done several times before. Except today, it hadn't been to welcome her in for a quiet evening together or a sunny afternoon on the deck with a glass of iced tea and Logan serenading her with a guitar. No, today he welcomed her into his home because of obligation she guessed. And that hadn't felt good at all.

She made the most of the evening, however, enjoying time with friends she hadn't seen in some time, eating tasty food—rumour told her that Stacy-Lynn could do more than sing, and celebrating a very exciting day for her sister. And the few times she stole glances of Logan or caught him looking at her, Sophie managed to tame her emotions. Those feelings would have to wait until another day. But what she couldn't ignore was the absence of life and shine in his eyes. The kind of light she saw every time they were together, especially when he had a guitar in his hands. It was obvious Logan was still in a dark struggle, waging war with events of his past. She just prayed that God would bring him through all of this to a place with life and shine and hope.

And that she would meet him there.

Nineteen

Sophie closed the final few buttons at the back of Anna's dress. With the sun shining through the sheer curtains soaking the dressing room with light and warmth, Sophie couldn't picture anything more perfect for her sister's wedding day. A light breeze followed the sun through the windows just enough to keep everyone cool amongst the hot curling irons and wardrobe changes. The forecast predicted comfortable summer temperatures and a few clouds to scatter the sky. No one could ask for anything better.

A few tears threatened to escape beneath Sophie's eyelids, and she blinked them away. With only half the day behind them, she felt enough emotion to last a month, maybe more, and she wouldn't trade any of it. It would be the only time she would get the honour of buttoning her baby sister into a beautiful white gown, so she would embrace all the feelings she could—all while trying to keep her make-up intact, of course.

She finished the last of thirty-six buttons, and spun Anna around. "All done."

Rita stood from her chair just a few feet away to survey her daughter. Their mother didn't worry about her make-up it seemed, because she let her tears fall freely. "Anna, you are absolutely radiant. Your dad is going to lose it." The three of them all chuckled in agreement. Jack was a tough man, far more than average, but when it came to his daughters, he was a softy. Completely.

"Drake, too," Sophie added.

Rita reached behind her to the vanity they had set up, and turned to face them with a veil laid across her arms. "One more thing."

Anna turned her back to Rita giving her easier access to her hair, which she had carefully pinned back leaving long blonde strands cascading down her back. The veil was long and sheer with large lace trim outlining the bottom edge. It complemented the dress perfectly. Rita clipped it in making sure it would stay secure for the rest of the day. "There."

"Gorgeous," Sophie whispered.

"Incredible," Rita added.

"Angelic," a voice sounded from the door.

The women turned to see their visitor and found Jack in the doorframe. He was already reaching for a tissue in the inside pocket of his suit jacket. "I'm supposed to give you girls the three minute warning and escort your mother to her front row seat."

Jack entered the room, hugged each of his daughters thoroughly, kissed Anna on the cheek with a promise to be right back, took his wife's hand and led her through the door. Sophie loved her father's hugs, and today's was extra special.

"Show time," Sophie said reaching for their bouquets. As she handed Anna the flowers, she noticed the bride was now tearing up.

"I just want you to know how much it means to have you stand next to me today," Anna whispered. "The world, Soph."

A tear spilled over, and that's all it took for Sophie's own to fall onto her cheeks. She reached for Anna, and they embraced. They forgot about the hair, the make-up, the bouquets and the dresses, and gave in to the moment. "Back at you. I love you so much."

A little more than a year ago, Sophie wasn't sure she would ever share a moment like this with her sister. With Anna living in Toronto and limiting the contact she had with her family because of her complicated past with Drake, Sophie barely had a relationship with her. And now they were sharing today together.

Jack sneaked through the door once again having swiftly ushered Rita to her seat. "Pastor Tim tells me it's time," he shrugged, "but I'm not sure if I'm ready to give my baby away." Before it had them all tearing up again, he added, "It's a good thing I have complete confidence in the man who's taking you from me to love you as much as I do."

A knock at the door hurried them into their places through the dressing room to stop behind the sanctuary doors to wait for the music to cue their entry. It didn't take long before Sophie heard the piano begin the introduction of one of Anna and Drake's favourite worship songs, *Afloat*. The lyrics paralleled what they overcame to be together, and today, as they become one.

Sophie watched as the ushers open the double doors and everyone in the pews stood to welcome the bride. The flower girls and ring bearer began their walk up the aisle as the first verse started. She clutched her bouquet close to her body and focused on the words. Even though Anna had chosen this song because it was a graceful reminder of how God reunited them, it was still one of

Sophie's favourites too. It gave hope during times of struggle, and even though today was not the day to focus on herself, Sophie reveled in the words just a moment longer.

The ocean's deep below my feet
Afraid of what's to come, so I slowly start to sink
I was waiting for my ending, But then You grab my hand
Just like I knew You would, You would

In that moment, Sophie felt a sense of comfort blanket over her, as if Jesus was right there beside her. She took a step toward the sanctuary and then another. Familiar faces filled row after row, pew after pew. The Coleman's—her and Anna's landlords—waved politely, Earl gave her an approving nod, and Mike sent a small smile her way. But none of those people held her attention. No, Sophie's eyes were transfixed towards the stage and on one of the men who stood there.

Logan looked so handsome in his suit. His hair was styled and not under a ball cap, his five-o'clock shadow was absent, in its place he was clean-shaven, and his hands were joined together in front of him. But she noticed one thing missing, the most important—his smile. Instead, Logan looked serious and focused. He looked like his job of being the best man was taking every ounce of concentration. And his eyes never met hers.

Sadness battled against the comfort she felt just moments before. It dawned on Sophie that she and Logan might never share a moment as special as this, and it almost broke her in two. The only thought that kept her gliding to the stage was words from one of her favourite verses. *For I know the plans I have for you… to prosper you…to give you hope and a future.*

Sophie clung to those phrases as she took the steps to her designated spot for the ceremony. God was in control of her future—their future. And His plans were for the best. And today, His plan was for her to be a witness of a miracle.

LOGAN pushed the food around on his plate. The prime rib dinner looked delicious, but he barely had an appetite. Since he was seated at the head table with just Drake, Anna, and Sophie, he guessed no one would notice if he didn't eat anything. Too much had happened today now his body was just as confused as his mind.

This morning before he was due at the church to get ready with Drake, Logan was invited for breakfast at his father's house. Stacy-Lynn and Lincoln had prepared his childhood favourite— a potato, bacon, and egg pan scrambler. He should have known they were trying to lure him in. But because he had just finished a grueling round of chores, was rather hungry, and was on a tight schedule, he went. While he ate, Stacy-Lynn sat quietly as Lincoln told Logan of their short-term plans. Stacy-Lynn was moving to Sethburn and would stay in her own apartment for the time being while she and Lincoln worked on their relationship.

Logan had objected immediately but not as forcefully as he did just days ago. Logan was beginning to understand he would need to come to terms with his mother being around, so he argued, but with much less vigor. His argument was losing steam, since he was up against too many other forces. Then his mother forged on. She told him about her encounter with God while attending church with a friend. The eye opening experience had solidified that she would never find the love she left behind when she began her music career, nor would she find it living a life run by agents, managers, and a security team. She admitted her mistake could not be undone, but she wanted to make an effort to build up their family again. Logan protested the idea, but Lincoln stood up for his mother and the plans they had made. He left Logan with powerful words.

"Son, remember you only get one mother, and we all only get one chance at true love. She's waving the white flag at both of us, and who are we to abandon her when she needs us most?"

If that wasn't enough to digest throughout the day, seeing Sophie walk up the aisle of the church was his undoing. She was *breathtaking*. Her hair was brushing her shoulders in natural waves, just a little blush graced her cheeks bringing out her summer tan and extenuating her gorgeous eyes. Her dress flowed to her knees moving with every step. But what one thing was missing—the light in her eyes. And Logan could only guess that he might have been the one to make it disappear.

So now, he sat at the head table after witnessing the joining of two people meant to spend their whole lives together in love, wishing that his own life was different. He wished that his childhood had been different, that maybe he could've done something more to keep his mother from leaving their family. He wished that he wouldn't have hidden his music from his parents, his friends, or Sophie for so long, suppressing the one thing that brought him joy while feeling down. He wished that he didn't live in fear that one day his adult life would replicate that of his childhood, that he and Sophie could build a life together without him wondering when the day would come when she had had enough. And he wished that he had the courage to give those fears over to the God his father and Sophie wholeheartedly trusted with their own lives.

But he couldn't change any of it so it seemed. Life was moving on and he couldn't keep up with it. He watched his best friend plan a future with his soul mate for the past year, and today, he witnessed them becoming one. He watched his parents over the last week reconnect as if what his mother did to them never even happened. He watched as Sophie laughed and danced with her sister tonight celebrating Anna and Drake's hopeful future as if she knew that whatever happened between them would be all right. Sophie would move forward with or without him, he real-ized, because that who she was. She was a strong, independent woman with faith that could move mountains, and even if the sadness he saw this morning was real, she would forge on.

And he didn't want her to.

All those things Drake mentioned just days ago at the auction—the times he shared with Sophie and the moments that he would miss if he walked away—came flooding back as Logan watched her join the conga line on the dance floor. He didn't want Sophie to have to move on without him and miss those times they had to look forward to while forgetting the ones they already shared. So why couldn't he take that chance?

Logan lifted from his chair ignoring his practically full plate. He needed some air. Within seconds he found an exit and pushed through the door. In his mind he knew Sophie was not like his mother—or who his mother used to be since apparently she'd made some changes. She wouldn't leave him without notice or a sudden change of heart. But in his own heart, his teenage self still ached at the loss and feared the time when he would feel that kind of pain again. The battle inside him was waging, and he wasn't sure who would conquer whom. But he was certain that he wished this war was over.

The coolness of the evening had settled in around the recep-tion hall as he took a seat on a bench along the sidewalk. Even with the loud music hyping up the dance floor, it was quiet enough outside that Logan could hear crickets and frogs in a pond close by. The stillness began to calm his mind the longer he sat.

The door of the hall opened slowly casting light and long shadows onto the lawn near the sidewalk. Lincoln appeared in the frame and stepped outside as he shut the door behind him.

His father sat beside him leaving the silence to fill the space between them. Minutes passed and Logan was grateful that

Lincoln had sensed his son was struggling. It felt like old times, even not so old times, when they could read each other and know when the other needed some company. Logan thought that he needed to be alone, but now with his dad by his side, he realized he was wrong.

"I'm scared, Dad," he said finally.

"I know, son."

Lincoln's arm draped across Logan's shoulders and he pulled him in close. Even though it was a gesture meant to comfort a child, Logan needed it as much as a man in a desert needed water, so he leaned into the support his father was offering.

"Aren't you scared to be with mom again?" Logan asked.

"There are moments, absolutely. But they pass as quickly as they come and in its place a sense of contentment settles in. It feels like coming home, but just with a little laundry to do before we can get comfortable, put our feet up, and relax."

Logan huffed at his father's analogy but understood the relevance all the same. He had some of his own laundry to do.

"Let me ask you something," Lincoln started, "When you watched Drake and Anna vow their lives to each other today, when you signed along the dotted line giving witness to those promises and thinking back to what it took for those two people to come together again and build the love they have, can you honestly tell me there was no divine intervention to make that happen?"

The question hit Logan square in the chest. Because he *absolutely* believed that all that had happened between Drake and Anna was not a coincidence. He just never thought of it like that before.

"I see the light's dawning there, son, so let me share somethin' else with you. I trust that God has that in store for *all of us*. A divine plan meant to better our lives so that we can live them to the fullest. He's got a plan for your mom and I to have this time, to figure it out, to pray about our relationship together and separately. And we'll know if it's goin' to work because it will or it won't—He'll show us."

"You think it's that simple, it's that easy to forgive?" Logan asked.

"A long time ago, I said those same vows to your mom that your best friend said to his wife today. I meant 'em then, and I mean 'em now. That never changed. So yeah, it's that easy with a little give and take."

"Mom wants me to forgive her."

"No doubt about that," Lincoln quipped, "but don't for a second think that what you're feeling is wrong. You were hurt, and she is responsible for that hurt. She knows it, and she wants to do what she can to soothe that pain because she's your mom *and* because she's the one who inflicted it. Know that I understand why you're angry, I had those very same days. But I will say that eventually, son, you *have to* let that go. It'll destroy you, it already ruined your past. It'll ruin your present, and I can guarantee it'll do worse to your future. You let go and let God, the rest is a breeze."

Logan huffed again unsure of the promises Lincoln was making even though it was all starting to make sense.

"Talk to your mom."

Logan would give his dad that. Absolutely. "Okay."

"Talk to your woman."

Logan sighed, leaned on his knees, and rubbed his face. "I don't think I have one anymore."

Lincoln gave Logan a tight squeeze. "The only thing holding you back from all that is you."

Twenty

Logan learned a lot in less than a day. And today, he was going to use some of his newfound knowledge. Starting with having a real and honest conversation with his mother. Since Lincoln now used text messaging, he sent his dad a message to send Stacy-Lynn over this morning once she was up and ready. And as Logan sleepily fiddled with the coffeemaker, he thought again of yesterday.

After the talk with his father outside the reception hall, Logan stayed on that bench a while longer before joining the party. It didn't take long for understanding to dawn on him. Finally, after a week of wrestling with every emotion, Logan was starting to feel that he had a handle on things. He was the one living in the past unwilling to move on and forgive, which meant it was due time for him to make some changes if he wanted any hope of moving forward, away from the hurt. And if he wanted a chance at convincing Sophie to look past his bullheaded ways of the last while, he needed to start at the beginning. What happened in his childhood was once in a lifetime—that was clear to Logan now. But what he also understood was that *Sophie* was also once in a lifetime—the opportunity of having her in his life was slipping through his fingers. And he needed to fix his relationship with Stacy-Lynn before he could mend the mess he made with Sophie. So the first order of business this morning was to brew some coffee and wait for his mother's knock on the door.

And he didn't have to wait long. Just as the clock on the microwave changed to eight o'clock, three taps sounded at the front door. Logan turned the knob and swung the door wide.

His mother had a guitar case in one hand and a steaming plate of muffins in the other.

"I brought breakfast," she said first thing. Logan couldn't tell if they were a peace offering, but he could tell they were blueberry—his favourite. He ignored the guitar case for the moment.

"I've got the coffee on. Come in," he motioned.

He poured two tall mugs and brought them along with the cream and sugar to the table while Stacy-Lynn plated the muffins and grabbed a few spoons.

They settled in and doctored their coffee. Now that she was here, Logan wasn't quite sure where to begin. He was hoping that maybe she would know where to start, since he assumed that Lincoln had filled her in on their conversation last night. He dug into his breakfast after two gulps of coffee and overthought everything he had gone over just minutes before in his head.

She must have sensed his uneasiness because she began the conversation. "Lincoln told me you wanted to talk. But he doesn't know how good my muffins are since I brought all that I made over here. So eat up—we've got some time."

Although it wasn't exactly a start to the difficult conversation they needed to have, it put Logan more at ease. He ate three muffins to her one before deciding he was finished and just needed to get on with it.

"I spent ten years hiding my music," he started. "I was scared that I would become what you did." He wasn't sure why he started with that, but it was one of the things weighing on his mind.

She reached for him. "Logan—"

"I was so angry that you left, I was angry that I had the same talent that took you away, I was angry that I couldn't share it because I was scared that one day it would change me like it changed you. But I did this summer for the first time."

He took a sip from his mug before continuing. "I made a ridiculous arrangement with a pretty girl in exchange for a date with her. Then I did something I never thought I'd do—I fell in love. Then I shared my music with her."

Stacy-Lynn's eyes welled up, emotion at the brink of overflowing. But Logan carried on. "She loved it, got as much joy out of it that I do even though I hid it all those years. She asked me to sing more, play another song, strum a little longer—we'd be on the deck and I'd just sit there and strum for hours. She convinced me to play on a stage, and I did it. I could feel the adrenaline pumping, I felt a rush watching the crowd dance to my music. But not once did I feel scared. Sophie was there, so I didn't need to be."

"I hope I'll get the chance to hear you play," she whispered while dabbing at her eyes.

"I don't know if I'll be able to play again," he said.

"Why not?"

"I have to get her back first. I don't think I could do it without her."

"You will, I know it," she reassured as she grasped his hand.

Logan drew comfort from his mother's touch for the first time in a decade. And he welcomed it. "I'm not afraid of it anymore though—it's a part of me just like it's a part of you."

"I didn't mean for it to hurt you. I'm so sorry." She wiped at the wetness on her cheeks.

"I know you are, Mom. But this last week I was fighting with myself whether or not to risk my heart again. You crushed it when you left, and I didn't know if I could ever live through something like that again."

"I'm not going to leave you again, I promise. I'll be around, I'll be here anytime you want to talk. I owe you a lot of years back, and I plan on making up all that time. Music never brought me near the amount of joy I had when I had you and your dad. You two are irreplaceable, I'm just sad it took me so long to figure that out."

"How did you?"

She smiled. "With a lot of help from above. I wouldn't be here if it wasn't for what God has been doing in my life lately."

"Tell me about it," he asked genuinely interested. If he wanted to piece everything back together, Logan also needed to figure out what he was going to do about God, too.

"My stylist, Gina, her and I became close over the past year or so. She's around my age, has a husband, two daughters. Her family was just so together, you know? It was so hard to watch her FaceTime her girls when we were on the road, say 'I love you' to her husband at the beginning and end of every call. Finally, I asked her how she did it. And her answer was so simple. She said 'with Jesus'."

Logan absently stirred his now cold coffee as he listened to the rest.

"It took me back to the days when I'd drop you off for Sunday school, and you'd come home and recite the verse you learned. I had that poster on the fridge and would add a sticker every time you learned a new one. Your dad would give you a high-five and we'd sit down to lunch after the service. Our family was so easy with Jesus on our side, and then I messed it all up. I knew after that conversation with Gina, I needed to make my way back to you."

"So you came back just like that?" Logan asked.

"I didn't. I needed to figure out who I was again with God. I went to church, and it was as if the message that day was meant just for me—a reminder of how God wants us to live being compassionate to one another, forgiving each other. And I couldn't help but wonder if you and your dad could look past my mistakes. That's when I came here. I wanted to live out that verse, because I had no doubt that you and your dad lived like that every day."

"It'll take some time for us to get back what we had," Logan admitted.

"I know, hun. I'll be the first to tell you that. But it's the best news that you are willing to give it a shot. Your dad will be so relieved, but me even more."

"I think dad wants it the most out of us all."

She chuckled. "You might be right."

Logan stood to clear their plates thankful that one hard conversation was over with. He felt lighter, happier about the whole situation. He had a long way to go to forgetting the past and rebuilding a close relationship with his mother, but now, he was officially on board. He had a lot of reservations about it, but he understood it was something his whole family needed. They needed to live out that scripture.

"I brought you something," Stacy-Lynn said as she entered the kitchen holding the guitar case he had forgotten all about.

He closed the dishwasher and waited for her to continue.

"It's the same guitar I used to play to you with." She set the case on the kitchen island and opened the top. The guitar caught the reflection from the window as she took it from the case. Logan remembered everything about that Gibson Les Paul acoustic, and he remembered the nights she would strum him to sleep with it.

"I used this to record my first album, play my first stadium, for every CMA Awards night, and in the back of my tour bus to write every single song I've ever recorded. I want you to have it."

Logan stood there staring at the instrument. This guitar had played a huge part in his childhood and an even bigger part on international stages. He felt honoured. "Are you sure?" he asked.

"Its first song was played for you and every song after that. It's yours, son."

Warmth moved through him from hearing her call him 'son', and he reached for it.

"I have an idea of what you can use this for," she said slyly.

"Oh yeah? What's that?"

"Yesterday, I watched a beautiful, blonde bridesmaid glance at you all night with a look of utter disappointment. It broke my heart a little bit. I think you might be able to cheer her up," she suggested.

Logan immediately checked his watch. If he hurried, he might make it in time. He set the guitar in its case and snapped it shut.

"Can I have a hug before you leave?" she asked with a smile.

He gladly embraced her, grateful for the gift and the idea. "Thanks, Mom."

"I love you, Logan."

He was out the door and into his truck in record time. But he managed to spare a few seconds to ensure that the guitar was secure in the back seat of his truck before driving away.

Then while barreling down the road towards town, Logan did what he hadn't done in a long time. He prayed.

SOPHIE reached for the snooze button on her phone. She needed a few more minutes before she would be able to face the day. As much as she was ecstatic for Anna and Drake, it had been a difficult day yesterday. Her sister had gotten married to the man of her dreams, and Sophie's future was looking rather bleak in that department.

During the reception and the few minutes she had to herself, Sophie had considered that she might have to change her rules on using her own profile with Match 'Em Up's database of clientele. It had been a moment of weakness that brought on a reminder that her relationship with Logan was almost nonexistent. The moment had come right before there was supposed to be a bridal party dance, which included Anna and Drake along with Sophie and Logan, when Logan slipped through the side door. The emcee had to rearrange the order of the evening's events because no one could locate the best man.

Would it really have been too difficult for Logan to explain that he just wasn't ready for a dance with her? Instead, Anna had done some subtle juggling and skipped over that dance all together to protect her. Sophie regretted that Anna had to miss out on a part of wedding tradition just because of an awkward situation caused by their best man.

And that was the moment when Sophie recognized that if she wanted to search for love, she might eventually have to look past the beautiful summer she had with Logan.

Sophie sat up on her bed checking the time. She had less than forty-five minutes before she would have to leave for church, which meant she'd have to hurry if she wanted a chance of being on time. Today was going to be a hard day no matter if she sat at home alone or carried on with her routine. And since Sophie wasn't a fan of self-pity, she slid her feet to the floor.

As she rushed through the shower and dressed for church, Sophie tried to push the words of yesterday to the back of her mind. Jessica, a friend of Anna's, had asked when she would be getting her own ring from the uncatchable bachelor. Mr. Coleman had joked with her about putting an ad in the paper about renting out the garage apartment because she would be soon to follow in the footsteps of her sister. Sheila had inquired about the amount of serenading that took place while dating Logan only after she gushed about seeing Logan on stage during the last mixer.

All the while, every time she caught a glimpse of her mother, Rita was looking at her with sadness and sympathy.

What had started out as a beautiful day of celebration had ended with Sophie crawling into bed with a headache and teary eyes. Today was a new day. There was no time like the present to be content being loved by an all-powerful God, two wonderful parents, her best friend and sister, and a new brother-in-law. Not to mention her many friends and clients. She wouldn't worry about tomorrow. And since it had been the theme of the week, Sophie retold herself that God's plan was perfect. And so was His timing.

She took the time to blow dry and style her hair since the past week's humidity seemed to be getting the best of her slight natural curl but skipped the make-up except for a bit of concealer to hide the darkness under her eyes. Her stomach didn't welcome the idea of breakfast, but she had to eat something or else the heat of the sanctuary would get to her in no time. Three ceiling fans did not cool an entire congregation in mid-summer heat.

She popped a bagel in the toaster and rinsed off a few fresh Saskatoon berries while waiting for her single cup of coffee to brew. She would definitely need the caffeine today. Once all of it was ready, she sat down at the small breakfast bar and pulled up the Facebook app on her phone.

Her news feed was filled with well wishes for Anna and Drake and tagged photos of the wedding festivities. A few people had tagged her in pictures from the ceremony, and even the photographer had managed to post a sneak peek of the happy couple. The photo of their first kiss as husband and wife was gorgeous, so she liked the photograph and added a congratulatory comment and a suggestion that this moment become a large canvas in their new home. The happiness emitted from the photograph eased Sophie's heartache just a little.

She slid her phone away and pulled her daily devotion book closer. Even running late, Sophie had time for a one-page encouragement while she finished her breakfast. Today's verse came for Psalm 32.

The Lord says, 'I will guide you along the best pathway for your life. I will advise you and watch over you.'

And while clutching that promise close to her heart, Sophie heard the strum of a guitar.

The End.